World War III

The Beginning

By

Joel M Fulgham

This book is a work of fiction. Places, events, and situations in this story are purely fictional. Any resemblance to actual persons, living or dead, is coincidental.

© 2000, 2003 by Joel M. Fulgham. All rights reserved.

No part of this book may be reproduced, stored in a retrieval system, or transmitted by any means, electronic, mechanical, photocopying, recording, or otherwise, without written permission from the author.

ISBN: 1-4107-6869-4 (e-book)
ISBN: 1-4107-6868-6 (Paperback)
ISBN: 1-4107-6867-8 (Dust Jacket)

This book is printed on acid free paper.

1stBooks - rev. 06/09/03

Introduction

After twenty-five years of development she was finally putting to sea. 'The world's most advanced nuclear submarine'. Bill Floyd started designing the magnetic flux propulsion system, "MFP", as a physics undergraduate in college. The major problem he encountered then was the power loss in normal conductor systems. In grad school, he worked on a modulated pulse generator, which he nicknamed "the cannon".

Bill then did a tour of duty in the Navy, learning the design and hands-on operation of a nuclear submarine. After eight years in the service, he obtained a job at the Marshall Research Center in Tennessee and perfected his "cannon" for the Army. His dream propulsion system, however, was still too expensive because it needed cryogenic superconductors to make the system operational. Luckily, another research group at the facility made a startling discovery-a superconductor that operated at a mere forty degrees Fahrenheit. This meant his MFP system could operate aboard a submarine. With his power problem solved, he formed a group to collaborate on the design of a submarine.

His supervisors did not believe the system would really work, so the group received meager funding. Although Bill was in charge of the entire group, he was mainly concerned with getting the cannon to work underwater and the final design for the propulsion system. Once the correct modulation and wavelength for penetrating water was found for the cannon, it was a snap to fit into a submarine. With his design completed and a working model built, he submitted the design to the Navy. After another year of design modification and battling for money, construction finally started. Two years later it was completed - the USS Hunley, SSNE 001. Roughly two-thirds the size of the aging Los Angles class attack submarines, the new armaments and fire control system made the Hunley more lethal. Its propulsion system and hull design made it virtually undetectable. And since this was her maiden voyage, the Navy allowed Bill to ride along to observe her performance first hand.

The familiar cigar shape of past submarines was now replaced by a flattened contour. Inside, it still maintained the familiar, three-deck layout forward of the reactor compartment, with the torpedo room amid-ship and tubes in both sides. The boat had a flat top and bottom and bulging sides. From the reactor to the stern, the top and bottom sloped toward each other, which reduced the internal compartments from three decks to two and eventually one. Once the internal compartment, or as submariners call it 'the people tank,' reached a height of five feet it ended. From there the hull contained storage tanks for essential lubrication and fuel oils.

As she departed from a submarine base along the northeast coast of the United States, all that was visible was the sail, a mere five feet above the water. The bulk of her two-hundred foot hull was five feet below the calm surface of the water. Any satellite, if any were still deployed, would mistake her for a small fishing boat.

Chapter 1

The moonless, midnight sky seemed darker than normal and the air had an eerie calm to it. The only disturbance of the river's surface was the slight ripple caused by the sail cutting through the water at 20 knots. The Captain was on the bridge taking her out for her maiden voyage, accompanied by Bill and two lookouts. The Captain finally broke the silence of the night, turned to Bill. "This new propulsion plant of yours is marvelous. We're making 20 knots using only 15% reactor power."

"Thank you, Captain. It took me a long time to work out all the bugs. I've dreamt of this day since the idea occurred to me high school. It'll give me a great deal of relief to find out if she'll actually perform to my expectations. With the MFP system and the newly designed hull, she should be able to outrun any warship and most torpedoes."

The intercom suddenly crackled to life, "Bridge, Sonar. We have a contact about 10,000 yards astern making thirty knots, designated as alpha one."

The Captain looked at Bill while reaching for the intercom, "Looks like we'll have open her up a little bit." Then pressing the button and leaning towards it, "Control room, this is the Captain, make speed thirty knots. Quartermaster, let me know when we have one-hundred-feet below the keel." The Captain released the switch, stood up and looked at Bill, "I'll give you another credit. Any other submarine would have a hard time hearing that sonar contact though the screw noise."

"That's just one of the advantages of magnet flux propulsion. Not only does it not mask sounds from astern, there's also no sound signature emitted to betray our presence, except at very high speed when there could be an unidentifiable swishing caused by the boat cutting through the water."

In a few seconds the intercom came to life again, "Conning tower, Control room. Maneuvering answering thirty knots, reactor power 21%."

Before the Captain could reply to the message Bill cut in, "Captain, if it's alright with you, I'm going below to check out the boat before we dive."

The Captain smirked, "You're not getting nervous about submerging, are you?"

"Not at all Captain, but why take chances? After all, she's a virgin," Bill replied with a wink.

As he climbed down the hatchway into the control room, he stole a quick glimpse at the Captain. Commander Helen St. Johns was the first female to command a United States submarine and, at thirty-seven, one of the youngest. She had previously served aboard three subs as a junior officer, two as executive officer and one other as commanding officer.

Of the five officers wanting this new boat, Commander St. Johns was the most junior and the only female. Surprisingly, none of the men objected to her being selected. Such was the respect she commanded from her peers in the silent service.

Helen was 5'8", 130 lbs. with lovely, light-brown hair and blue eyes, though not a striking beauty, her face exuded warmness that could make anyone feel comfortable around her. Her eyes betrayed the incredible inner strength and wisdom she possessed.

Helen grew up in Charleston, South Carolina and learned to love going to the beach at an early age. The first summer after her thirteenth birthday, her father began taking her to sea on his shrimp boat. It was then that she realized it wasn't the beach she loved, but the sea itself. The salt spray carried by the wind over the bow of the ship and her feeling of how small she was compared to the vastness of the sea, combined to fill her with the thrill of life. Now despite the fact she had been away from home for fifteen years, she managed to maintain her southern charm and temperament. Bill witnessed that charm. In the year-and-a-half they knew each other, she had always kept her cool, even when confronted with frustrating situations.

Bill toured every compartment on the boat, checked every gauge and meter he could remember. He talked to every person on watch, inquiring if they had noticed anything out of the ordinary since getting underway. Finally, satisfied that everything was working correctly, he started back toward the control room when the familiar announcement came over the loudspeakers, the one that always made his stomach tighten, "Dive, Dive", followed by the harsh sound of the klaxon. As Bill arrived at the control room, Helen came down the ladder and turned to the diving officer, "Dive, take her down, make your keel depth six-zero feet. Up scope. Navigator, are we in the center of the channel?"

The Navigator glanced at the Fathometer, "Yes Ma'am, the bottom is one hundred ten feet and slowly dropping away."

Stepping up onto the raised portion of the control room, she flipped the switch labeled SONAR, "Sonar, this is the Captain. Keep a close eye on the forward scan sonar, I don't want to bump into anything our first time out. And what's the story on Alpha One?"

A female voice replied, "Captain, Sonar. Alpha One is still at 10,000 yards astern making thirty knots but veering off the channel and opening the angle, it will be out of range shortly. Side and forward scan sonar, show all clear."

Helen moved to the periscope, grabbed both handles and pulled them down. She pressed her eyes into the eyepieces and spun around in a three-hundred-sixty-degree circle. Satisfied no other ships were in the area, she stepped back and turned to the young officer next to her. "Lieutenant Gorecki, you now have the Conn as Officer of the Deck. Make your speed twenty knots and keep the bottom fifty feet below the keel until we reach a depth of two hundred feet. Maintain a heading of one-seven-zero until we reach checkpoint Able. XO, you and Mr. Floyd please join me in the wardroom."

The XO was barely able to get the words "yes, Ma'am" out before she was gone. He and Bill looked at each other and shrugged. The XO spoke, "I guess she means now. Care to follow me?"

Bill replied, "Why not? Lead on McDuff". They both laughed.

The XO, Lieutenant Commander James Thomas, was unusually tall for submarine duty. Standing fully erect he was 6'4". And he seldom was able to stand up straight in the boat. He had dark brown hair and a muscular build. His size earned him instant respect from the crew, but during the final fit-out of the boat, his personality and actions gained him a lot more than that. Bill had witnessed James crawling into the bilges to assist crewmembers working in hard-to-reach areas. This Executive Officer, normally the most-hated officer on board, had treated this crew with respect and as equals. The crew had, in return, given him unwavering loyalty. James expected the boat's other officers to also lend a hand performing the arduous work of getting the boat ready for sea. This attitude irritated the other officers who felt they were above that and should not have to crawl around in the bilges.

As Bill and James entered the wardroom, Helen was sitting at the head of the table, perusing some papers. The men sat down as the mess cook produced three cups of coffee. Helen waited until the cook left, then reached into her shirt pocket and pulled out a folded sheet of paper. "This will only take a minute. I would like to go over tomorrow's schedule. At 0800, we will engage in cat-and-mouse games with the destroyer, USS Key, one hundred miles past checkpoint Able. The Key knows precisely where we will enter their sector, so they will have their sonar focused directly on us for short while. Jim, this will be a long day, so breakfast should be at 0530 and secured by 0645. That will give the galley time to rig for silent running. At 0650 rig the boat for deep submergence. We'll take her down to seven hundred feet and verify watertight integrity. This will give us room to maneuver for the games. Then we'll find a thermal layer and take up a position just below it and rig for silent running. I want all this accomplished by 0730. If we have not been detected by 0900, we'll surface one hundred yards off the Key and verify contact with underwater radios, then submerge again and finish deep submergence test and speed trials. Any questions or comments?"

James spoke. "Yes Ma'am. Can we station the torpedo fire control and tracking party for shot setup practice before we go to the practice range for qualification?"

"Sure, Jim, why not. If that's all, let's turn in. We have a busy day ahead, starting in four hours. Oh, Bill, I would like you to stay in engineering tomorrow, so you can monitor the reactor's performance."

"Okay, Captain, see you in the morning." With that, the trio retired. The Captain went to her stateroom and Bill followed to the XO's cabin next to hers. Both shared a common head. James went down a deck to officers' country, where he was sharing a stateroom with another officer. It didn't take long for all three to fall asleep.

Chapter 2

Bill became aware of someone knocking on his door. After several raps, he managed to open his eyes and respond that he was awake. He sat up and oriented himself. Once his eyes were able to focus, he looked over at the clock mounted at the foot of his bunk. It read 0545. "Oh, Shit. This is too early to start work," he mumbled to himself, then struggled to his feet and stumbled into the head. After dressing, he made his way to the wardroom for breakfast. By the time he arrived, the officers coming off watch were already eating and after exchanging a few pleasantries, the meal was finished in almost complete silence.

After breakfast and three cups of coffee, Bill made his way to the control room just in time to hear the Officer of the Deck order the Diving Officer to bring the boat up to one-fiver-zero-feet and deploy the floating antenna wire. This was to be the Hunley's last scheduled radio contact until after the morning's test. Almost immediately, the speaker crackled to life, "Conn, Radio. We're receiving an urgent message from COMSUBLANT."

"Very well" answered the Officer of the Deck, who turned to the cluster of phones on the bulkhead behind her, picked up the one with a push button dial and punched in the number, one.

After several rings a voice came over the line, "This is the Captain."

"Excuse me, Captain. This is the Officer of the Deck. We're receiving an urgent message from COMSUBLANT."

"Thank you, Ensign. Inform radio I'll be there shortly."

"Yes Ma'am." The Ensign placed the receiver back in its cradle, turned back to the intercom box and depressed the radio button, "Radio, Conn. Captain's on her way."

"Damn, we just left port. What the hell could have happened already?" The Diving Officer asked aloud.

"I bet somebody in the Republic sneezed again," replied the young seaman at the helm.

Idle gossip filled the room until the Captain stuck her head in through the hatch. "Officer of the Deck. I want all off-duty officers in the wardroom in five minutes. Continue with the plan of the day, rig for deep submergence and take her down. I want you to deploy the Deep Water Radio Receiver and verify that it's receiving."

"Aye, aye," was all the Ensign got out before Helen was gone.

Ensign Crockett, the Officer of the Deck, picked up the microphone for the ship's announcing system. "All off-duty officers muster in the wardroom in five minutes. Rig ship for deep submergence. Make status reports to the Conn pronto." As she hung up the mike, she turned to the Diving Officer, "Dive, report when stations are manned and ready."

As the crew prepared to take the boat down, Bill leaned against the bulkhead in the corner of the room out of everyone's way. He contemplated the state of world affairs, affairs shaky enough to finally convince the Navy and Congress to build this new submarine.

After the fall of the Soviet Union, world governments let their guard down and in an attempt to cut defense spending, finally eliminated nuclear weapons. But they also came up with some rather questionable treaties.

One was outlawing spy satellites, which made everyone blind to what was happening in world hot spots. Then the Arab countries united to form the Islamic Republic. Only Saudi Arabia attempted to hold out, but their ruling government was overthrown by revolution. The radical sect behind the revolt eagerly joined the Republic.

Now with the wealth they had acquired from the sale of oil, they bought surplus military equipment from the cash-poor, former communist-bloc countries, including ships, subs, tanks, fighters and bombers. The result was the creation of the world's largest military force.

Israel was now completely surrounded by united, hostile forces that continually threatened to violate the treaty that had brought an uneasy peace to the region twenty years earlier. So far, however, the Republic had taken no aggressive action. Israel, on the other hand, continued buying war material from U.S. defense industries, which kept the American companies operational despite the lack of new purchases by the U.S. government. The latest estimates from Israel speculated that half the population of the country was involved is some form of the military. Even with this staggering percentage, they were still no match for the gigantic military of the Republic.

The former countries of NATO now controlled the northern Mediterranean and Straits of Gibraltar. The Islamic Republic controlled the eastern and southern Mediterranean, including the Suez Canal. With the fall of the Soviet Union, the European countries requested the United States to remove all troops from their territories. The US complied to help it's own budget constraints, but retained port-of-call rights in most counties more for economic than military reasons. With the troop removal came the fall of NATO and the beginning of the ETO, the European Treaty Organization, a financial arrangement rather than a military agreement.

Bill was brought out of his deep thoughts by the announcement that all stations reported manned and ready.

In an almost uncaring voice, the young Officer of the Deck replied, "Very well. Dive, take her down to five hundred feet."

"Aye, Aye, Ma'am."

"Planesman, establish a ten degree down bubble. Chief of the watch, pump out 5000 pounds." As the depth gauge approached four hundred feet, Bill looked around the Control room and saw different expressions on the faces around him. The men and women who had served on other boats looked relaxed, while those on their first deployment showed apprehension.

Finally, the old Senior Chief, standing watch as Diving Officer, ordered the Planesman to zero the bubble and the sub stopped precisely at five hundred feet. "Officer of the Deck, we are at five hundred feet and steady."

"Very well, Phone talker, have all compartments check for leaks."

A few minutes later, the Phone talker announced, "All compartments report no leaks."

As they continued in steps down to six and then seven hundred feet, the faces on the new submariners showed greater fear while the old-timers continued with the same, unconcerned looks. This was actually the first time Bill had a chance to stand back and observe a crew in this situation. He wondered if the seasoned submariners, held their expressions from having done this before or merely from practice and not showing their true feelings. When at seven hundred feet, it was reported that the boat's watertight integrity was intact; Bill personally felt a great deal of relief and satisfaction that the boat had passed this part of the test.

The wardroom

Helen addressed the officers gathered there, "As you already heard, we received a message from COMSUBLANT directed to all boats currently at sea. The message reads:

> Informational Alert. An SR-75 flying over the southern Indian Ocean has spotted a large Islamic Republic battle group moving south toward Cape Horn. Destination unknown. Intent unknown. Continue present operation.

"There's probably nothing to this, but this is the first time the Republic has sent a fleet around the cape and Washington is concerned. Since this is probably a false alarm, I wish this information to remain in the wardroom. No need getting the crew excited about this. However, to be on the safe side, I want a report from each division, listing requirements for battle readiness. And I want them in two hours. XO, please inform the officers on watch that I will expect their reports two hours after they are relieved. That is all. Dismissed."

Control room

The Officer of the Deck made the announcement to secure from deep submergence, rig boat for silent running, station the torpedo fire control and tracking party. Pressing the intercom for the sonar shack, she asked the sonar chief what depth they needed for the best thermal layer. Bill looked at his watch. 0725, right on the Captain's time table. The officers who had been in the meeting with the Captain now seemed to be a bit edgy. Bill couldn't help but wonder what the Captain told them.

"Conn, Sonar. There's a pretty good thermal layer at 535 feet."

The Officer of the Deck replied, "Very well,' then looked toward the Diving Officer, and directed him to bring the boat up to 590 feet.

Since Bill would not be needed for this part of the games, he headed back to his stateroom. One of the requirements for silent running is for all off-watch personnel to turn into their racks. As he passed the Captain's stateroom, he noticed her sitting at her fold down desk, reading a stack of papers. He stuck his head in and said, "so far, so good."

She looked up at him, quizzically. "Are you sure the cannon will work?"

"I see no reason why not, it worked in all the tests, but I'll feel better once it's tested at the range. Why do you ask?" Bill queried.

"Bill, what I'm about to tell you is confidential. We have to be absolutely sure that it will work. You see, before we left port I was informed that at least three unidentified submarines had crossed the Coastal sonar array. Their continued headings would have positioned them off Jacksonville, Norfolk and Groton. The Navy is conducting search operations to locate their current positions and Naval Intelligence speculates they are here to spy on ship movements. Those subs are somewhere between Andros and us. Since we're carrying only practice torpedoes, the cannon is the only effective weapon we have. I don't want to get caught with our pants down."

"Since it's that important, maybe the Key will allow us a practice shot at one of their launches. They could tie the wheel and let it run while we do a shot setup and actual firing test."

"Good idea. I'll take it up with the Key's captain when we surface."

"Helen, now it's my turn to ask questions. What the hell is going on? Ever since your meeting in the wardroom the officers are acting strange."

"I can't tell you any more right now, Bill, but when I can, I'll fill you in. For now, why don't you go down to the cannon control room and run a systems check with the fire control tech. I'll tell the Officer of the Deck you have my permission to conduct tests."

"Yes Ma'am." Bill left and headed to the bow compartment. The cannon uses a superconducting magnet to store electrical energy.

When fully charged, energy is released in one pulse to a microwave generator that creates a single pulse of microwaves at a wavelength that penetrates water up to 4000 yards. Once the pulse reaches the target, it reacts with the material in it to generate tremendous heat and either melts the hull of a ship, or at least weakens it. Unfortunately, this is a very close-range weapon and can only be fired at 45 degrees off the bow. Another limitation is that it requires three minutes to prepare for another shot, this time allows components to cool and the magnet to recharge.

Chapter 3

0730 The Pentagon. Meeting of the Joint Chiefs of Staff

"Gentleman, the last report on the Republic's carrier group is that it will reach the Cape tonight. Also, Israel has reported a carrier group left Beirut yesterday afternoon, heading west. The French carrier, Bonaparte, sighted a group of transports running maneuvers off the coast of Libya two days ago. We also had a report from Australia about Republic warships around the Solomon Islands. Does anyone have an idea of what they might be up to?"

"I think you're just looking to find a problem, Mike. They're probably running more maneuvers, trying to get us all fired up," piped up Marine General Robert Walton.

Air Force General John Freeman added, "There doesn't appear to be anything consistent in these operations. At least not consistent with any of the scenarios we've considered as a first act of aggression from the Republic. Therefore, I have to agree with Bob."

Admiral Steve Schmidt, the intellectual of the group, studied what had been suggested before speaking up, "General, I tend to agree, to a degree, with Bob and John. Those submarines that crossed the costal sonar array do have me puzzled, though. They're watching our major ports for a reason, but damned if I know why. I'm also not prepared to speculate as to what they're up to, but I would recommend following them with caution. It might be a good idea to fill in the White House."

General Mike Wish, chairman of the joint chiefs, studied the other three men and thought for several minutes before speaking again. "Gentlemen, I, too, agree that there is not much to go on here, but I also agree that the White House should be appraised of the situation. I will arrange to meet with the President and the Secretaries of State and Defense and let ya'll know when. Meanwhile, John, have your boys run diagnostics on our satellites to make sure they're operable in case we need to launch them. If the Republic is really up to something, an act of war on their part will negate the satellite treaty. I would also like all of you to bring me numbers on battle readiness. I realize that during the last two decades, the budget cuts have left us with little more than a token military and we are not in shape to mount a defense, much less an offensive. Even though the politicians and public would not listen to our warnings that peace is not an easy state to achieve, let alone maintain, they've been still unwilling to pay the high of peace. We must do whatever is necessary to protect our shores against hostile forces. So, if there are no other questions or comments, I suggest you make preparations for the meeting with the President. Good Day."

As the others left the room, General Wish sat his large, muscular body down in one of the plush chairs and spun around so he could study the world map on the wall. He was totally consumed with noting the locations of the Republic's fleets and trying to figure out their destinations and purposes. Mike Wish had been a young Lieutenant back when President Bush ordered troops to Saudi Arabia. Now he was the Chairman of the Joint Chiefs of Staff, facing another foe that possessed a military that dwarfed his own. The U.S. had no forwardly deployed forces and little capability of moving ground forces in short order. The Navy had been the only branch of service to maintain a short-notice, limited-attack capability. However, even the Navy's six carrier groups would be no match for the seventeen or eighteen carrier groups of the Republics. "If they decide to fight, how can we possibly buy enough time to stop them?" the General thought.

USS Hunley

"Secure from silent running." came over the P.A. system at 0855. Bill was just finishing the systems check on the cannon fire control system and answering questions from the tech that would be responsible for its maintenance. "Well, Petty Officer Hein, if there's nothing else, I better report to the Captain."

"No sir. Thank you for clarifying those things for me."

"Please call me Bill, officers are sirs."

Bill left the small compartment at the bow of the boat and headed down the narrow passageway past the officer's quarters and wardroom. He climbed up the stairs to the upper level where the control room, radio and sonar shacks, the Captain's and XO's staterooms were. After knocking on the Captain's door and receiving no answer, he headed for the control room. As he entered, he heard, "Dive, bring us to periscope depth, ahead one-third."

"Periscope depth, ahead one-third, aye, Ma'am." repeated the Dive who began issuing the complicated orders that followed that simple command.

In a few minutes the Dive called out. "Officer of the Deck, we are at periscope depth and holding."

"Very well, raising scope one." Then, proceeding with the customary three-hundred-sixty-degree turn, the young Officer of the Deck settled on the only object in sight. "Captain, I have the Key, one-hundred yards to port."

"Very well. Put us on the surface."

The young officer picked up the 1MC microphone and announced, "Prepare to surface without air, Diving Officer, surface."

The Dive took over, "Close all vents, full rise on the planes." Immediately everyone felt the boat push her way to the surface. After a short silence the Diving Officer spoke up, "Officer of the Deck, the sail is above the surface."

"Very well, Dive." The Lieutenant then made the announcement, "all stations, prepare to ventilate." In only a few minutes all stations reported they were ready to ventilate. "Dive, start the blower on all main ballast tanks." The big blower started up and forced air into the ballast tanks, which in turn, forced the water out. With the water removed from the ballast tanks the ship was lighter than the water she displaced and remained close to the surface with only the sail to betray her location.

"Station lookouts. Dive, I am moving to the bridge."

Helen moved to the intercom and pushed the radio button, "Radio, this is the Captain. Contact the Key and request a launch to transport me. I'll be topside, waiting"

"Yes Ma'am," came back over the intercom.

"Dive, inform the Officer of the Deck I'm coming topside and that the Key should be sending over a launch."

A few seconds later she emerged from the hatch onto the bridge, "Welcome Captain. It sure is a beautiful day."

"I can't argue that, Lieutenant. Being underwater for months at a time sure makes you appreciate days like this."

"Here comes my launch. Lieutenant, while I'm gone, finish checking all communications and rig the boat for full deep submergence and angles and dangles by 1000 hours. Be ready to get under way as soon as I get back."

"Aye, Aye Ma'am" the Lieutenant snapped. The launch pulled alongside the sail and the Captain went over the side into it.

0958

"Welcome back, Captain. Communication systems have been checked out. We're rigged for deep submergence."

"Very well. Have the laser fire control tracking party stationed. Contact sonar and have them track the target ten degrees off the port bow at one hundred fifty yards, moving away. Designate it 'Delta 1'. Also have Mr. Floyd lay to the cannon fire control station."

While waiting for the crew to assemble at their stations, Helen announced over the PA system. "I wish to take this opportunity to inform you that the Captain of the Key said they had no idea we were in the area until we surfaced. So congratulations on a job well done."

As she finished, "Bridge, Conn. All stations manned and ready," came over the intercom.

"Lieutenant, don't take this personally." Helen spoke into the mike again, "Conn, Bridge. This is the Captain. I have the conn. Helm, come left ten degrees, make speed five knots. Laser control, target the top of the pole above the target dead ahead and fire when ready."

"Aye, Aye," came the reply and five seconds later a bright light appeared at the top of the pole. In what seemed like slow motion, the top tumbled into the water.

"Well done, Seaman Johnson, secure your station and lay below. "Clear the bridge." The three others topside scurried down the hatch, leaving Helen alone to survey the open water and beautiful clear, blue skies. After checking the location of the target launch one more time she looked at her watch as she ordered, "Crash dive, all ahead standard!" With that, she dove down the hatchway, closed the hatch and spun the wheel to lock it.

At the bottom of the ladder, she heard, "We are green across the board. All main ballast tank vents are open."

"Very well chief, ten degrees down on the forward planes." As the depth gage reached sixty feet, the Diving Officer continued his series of orders, "Full dive on the planes." The deck immediately slanted forward fifty degrees and the boat's depth increased rapidly.

As they passed one-hundred-fifty-feet, the Captain spoke up, "Thirty seconds, very good. Dive, level off at three-hundred-feet and ring up ahead one-third. XO, come up with firing solution for the target identified by sonar as Delta 1."

Within moments the XO responded, "We have a solution, Captain."

"Very well, feed it to the cannon fire control."

"Aye, Aye, Ma'am." The man then flipped several switches. "Captain, the cannon computer has the solution."

"Very well. Open the cannon doors."

"Aye, Aye. Opening cannon door." The XO reached up, toggled the door switch and waited for the indicator light to change from red to green. "Cannon doors open."

Helen turned to the XO, "Fire the cannon."

"You mean, actually blow it out of the water?"

"That's what I said." Helen replied with irritation in her voice.

"Yes Ma'am," James continued to look at Helen, waiting for a cancellation order and patted the chief at the console on his shoulder. "Chief, commence firing."

The Chief pushed the button that sent the firing signal to cannon fire control. The lights dimmed briefly and a loud pop echoed through the boat. The cannon fired.

"Conn, Sonar. We have a loud explosion dead ahead. Target bearing zero degrees relative has disappeared" came over the intercom speaker.

Helen pressed the intercom switch for the radio room, "Radio, this is the Captain. Ask the Key for a report on the target, then relay the report to the crew. Officer of the Deck, you have the conn. Continue the deep submergence test in increments of 100 feet down to 1500 feet. Once that is completed, bring us back up to 1000 feet, and take us up to 75 percent reactor power. Do some course and depth changes. If everything checks out, proceed to ahead flank, 100 percent reactor power and more maneuvers. I'll be in my stateroom. Have Mr. Floyd come to my cabin"

As Bill headed to the Captain's cabin, an announcement come from over the intercom, "Attention crew, the test firing of the cannon was successful. The Key reports the target was completely destroyed. Congratulations."

Bill reached Helen's cabin. She sat at her desk reading and when he knocked on her door she motioned for him to take the chair against the bulkhead. He sat and waited for her to finish what she was reading. Helen finally put the material down and looked at him with her brilliant blue eyes, "I see the cannon worked well."

"Yep. However, the pop from the magnet discharge was a little louder than I'd anticipated. If I can use a couple of warm bodies, I believe we can dampen the sound a bit."

"I'm glad you said that. A noise that loud would surely give our position away. I'll have the engineer provide two bodies. Will that be enough?"

"I think so. Shall I start now or go to engineering to observe the boat's performance?"

"I think the cannon has the higher priority, don't you? How long will this modification take?"

"About eight hours"

Back on the Conn

"Officer of the Deck, we are at 1500 feet. All stations report no leaks."

"Very well. Radio, inform the Key our watertight integrity test were satisfactory. Messenger, inform the Captain. Dive, bring us to 1000 feet, ring up ahead full."

"Yes, Sir. Helm, twenty degree up bubble." As the boat slowly rose and reached 1050 feet, the Dive ordered, "Helmsman, zero your planes. Officer of the Deck, boat's depth 1000 feet, maneuvering answering ahead full, boat's speed 62 knots, reactor power 50%."

"Very well, Dive, how's she handling?"

The Dive leaned over and asked the two seaman sitting at the helm and planes if they had noticed any change in the controls, then turned to the Officer of the Deck, "No problems so far."

Joel M. Fulgham

"Very well. Bring reactor power to 75%. If any handling problems occur, let me know immediately." The young Lieutenant reached for the microphone and pressed the button for maneuvering, "Maneuvering, Conn. Slowly increase speed to 75% reactor power."

"Conn, maneuvering, slowly increasing speed to 75% reactor aye." A few minutes later, "Conn, maneuvering, answering 75% reactor power."

"Diving Officer, mark ship's speed."

"87 knots, sir!"

"Okay now, let's see how she handles. Bring us up to 800 feet, heading of 275 degrees."

The Dive took a look at the two seaman sitting at the helm and dive planes. Both were holding the controls so tight, their knuckles had turned white. "Relax you two, this is nothing you haven't done before, it's just a little faster. Now, bring the planes up ten degrees and the rudder right ten degrees to a new heading of 275." Immediately, the boat shot up and banked hard right. "Bring the controls to zero, now!" The Dive commanded trying to remain calm but his trembling voice betrayed him. Once the boat resumed it's level course the Dive surveyed the instruments to determine where they were. "Officer of the Deck, we are at 725 feet heading two-eight-five."

"Is everyone all right," asked the young Lieutenant as he attempted to get back to his feet.

Before anyone could reply, Captain St. Johns came running in through hatch. "What the hell just happened?"

"Ma'am, we are at 75% reactor power, speed is 87 knots. We attempted to change depth and heading. The Diving Officer ordered ten degrees on the planes and rudder. Well then, you felt result."

"Are we at the ordered depth and heading?"

"No Ma'am."

"Then make the corrections using only five degree changes on the planes and rudder"

"Y—Yes Ma'am," stuttered the Officer of the Deck, as Helen turned to leave. Once she left the control room, the Lieutenant looked at the Diving Officer. "You heard the lady, get there, slowly!"

"Yes Sir. Planes down five degrees, left rudder two degrees steady on course 275." This time the boat only nosed down slightly as she descended back down to 800 feet. "Zero your planes. Officer of the Deck, we are at 800 feet on a heading of 275 degrees."

"Very well." He pressed the button again, "Maneuvering, increase speed to ahead flank, 100% reactor power."

The Engineering Officer retorted, "Only if you don't make any wild course adjustments again. Increasing to ahead flank, 100% reactor power."

Within a few minutes the intercom came alive, "Officer of the Deck, Maneuvering, we are answering ahead flank, reactor power 100%. We have speed as 108 knots."

"Dive, mark your speed."

"Sir we also have 108 knots."

"Damn, we did it," murmured the Lieutenant as the Captain came back into the control room and walked up behind the Diving Officer.

"Not bad," she said turning to the Officer of the Deck. "Now bring us to course 180, depth 1400 and slow to a standard bell, in that order. Got it Lieutenant?"

"Yes Ma'am. Dive, come left to course 180, take her down to 1400 feet."

"Aye, aye sir. Planes down five degrees, helm, five degrees left rudder and come to course 180." At this speed the boat quickly came to the new heading and depth. "Officer of the Deck, current heading, 180, depth, 1400. Ringing up ahead standard. Maneuvering replies ahead standard. Reactor power coming down, speed decreasing."

"Lieutenant, call for an emergency stop."

The officer gave the Captain a questioning look as he reached for the mike and made the announcement, "Emergency stop, deploy the water brakes."

The Chief of the Watch jumped up and pressed a red knob at the end of his console. "Water brakes deployed sir." The rapid deceleration caused by the two big pieces of metal being pushed out hydraulically from the sides of the boat caused several people to fall and suffer bruises. "Speed is zero sir, pulling in the water brakes."

Joel M. Fulgham

"Officer of the Deck, pass me the mike." Helen took it and spoke to the crew, "This is the Captain. I hope this morning's sea trials have not inconvenienced anyone too much. They have been necessary; for our missions may require the use of any of the maneuvers we did this morning. We have one more test to perform this morning, one that many people have found enjoyable, the emergency blow. We'll be starting at 1400 feet, so it should be a fun ride and spectacular finish." Helen handed the mike back to the Officer of the deck as she continued, "Officer of the Deck ring up ahead two-thirds, clear the top with sonar and have radio inform the Key we are going to perform the blow."

"Yes Ma'am. Radio, inform the Key. Sonar, do you have any contacts ahead or above us?"

"All clear except for the Key 10,000 yards astern."

"Very well, Ring up ahead two-thirds."

"Already done, sir. Answering two-thirds."

"Dive, hit the chicken switch."

"Yes sir," replied the Dive reached for the switch to active the blow. The sound of high-pressure air being released into the ballast tanks roared through the boat. Then the boat gave a shudder and slowly began to rise. As the water was displaced she began to climb faster and faster.

On board the Key, the view was magnificent as the Hunley broke the surface of the water at about 45 degrees. Her vertical speed pushed her three quarters of the way out of the water before she slammed back down with a tremendous splash. The submarine now sat high on the surface, her hull exposed, since the emergency blow entirely emptied the tanks that normally kept the hull submerged.

A message was immediately received over the underwater phones, "Hunley, this is the Key. Beautiful! If you do not require our services any more we'll be taking off, other duties to perform, you know."

"Key, this is the Hunley. Thanks for your help. We'll take it from here. We have an appointment too."

A smiling Helen ordered, "Maneuvering, commence charging air banks. Diving Officer, make our speed 30 knots, continue heading of 180."

"Lieutenant, you and the crew performed admirably this morning. Pass that on to the crew. Navigator, plot a course to the coastal sonar array, let's see if they can detect us."

"Hi Bill, I hope we didn't make it too rough on you down here," Helen said as she entered the bow compartment.

"We could have done without the emergency stop. One of my helpers fell and cut his hand pretty good. He's gone to see the corpsman. The emergency blow was a lot of fun, though. I've never experienced one from the bow before."

"Do you need a replacement for the injured man?"

"No thanks. The hard part's done. Now it's just a matter of getting these damping shields in place. We'll manage."

"Okay then. By the way, we topped off at 108 knots, but we can't exceed five degrees on steering surface at higher than a full bell."

"Then we'll have to work on that."

"Is there something that can be done to correct the problem?"

"I think so, but it will require going into dry dock, so don't count on it too soon."

Chapter 4

1400 hrs The White House situation room

"Mr. President, the Islamic Republic has deployed at least four groups outside their normal deployment areas, as well as having a number of transports exercising off Libya."

"So? What would you like me to do about it? Tell them they are not allowed to leave their normal patrol areas."

"Of course not, Sir. We just feel they may be up to something and you should know about it. However, you can politely contact their embassy and inquire what their intentions are."

"You're right, I can do that. But that can be misconstrued as interfering in their right to the seas, which I am not prepared for at this time."

"Then, will you at least support moving a carrier group to the east coast of England?"

"No! I won't take any action that could cause a misunderstanding. For now we'll do nothing. Understood?"

"Yes sir. Sorry for wasting your time." General Wish led the other officers from the room.

Once in the van headed back to the pentagon General Wish was concerned. "Steve, what's the status of the carrier groups?"

"The Reagan is in the North Atlantic with three cruisers, four destroyers, nine frigates and three subs. The Bush is anchored off Fort Lauderdale with her escorts scattered in ports up and down the Southeast coast. The Enterprise II is in dry dock for at least six more months. The Lincoln is in the North Pacific with five cruisers, six destroyers and two submarines. The Roosevelt is in Pearl and the Truman's about ready to come out of the yards."

"That's great. Six carriers against the Republic's eighteen. And worse, we only know where four of them are. Freeman, what's your status?"

"Not much better I'm afraid, we have a total of eleven operational fighter wings, five on the east coast and six on the west. We also have, two bomber groups, one on each coast. We could reactivate five fighter wings and two bomber groups in six weeks if needed."

"General Walton, your Marines?"

"We could deploy about 50,000 troops, all heavily armed and ready for action, plus 100 helicopters for close ground support."

"The Army can deploy 20,000 infantry, two armored divisions, six artillery divisions and two tank division as well as support groups, within three days, two times that in four weeks. The problem is getting them where they're needed."

"The Navy has only six active 'gator freighters' for deploying the marines, General. We could probably get six more ready in a month by cannibalizing other ships that can't get underway."

"The Air Force has two airlift commands of twenty-five C-5 galaxies, each. We still maintain some starlifters, but I'm not sure how many are operational."

"Steve, how long will it take to get the Bush underway?"

"Two days."

After deep thought, General Wish said, "Admiral, get the Bush's carrier group underway. Have them patrol the East coast and find those subs. Have the Roosevelt prepare for getting underway, but do not deploy. Let's also get enough subs out to observe the enemy's movements. But don't get caught!"

"General, if we deploy additional subs while theirs are sitting outside our ports, they may get suspicious. We can accomplish the same objective by redeploying our subs already at sea."

"Do you have enough to do the job without short-changing the carriers?"

"Yes. We have one in the south Atlantic that can intercept the force coming round the cape and get a better idea of its size. We also have one in the Med that can move close enough to observe the transports. Finally, we have the Hunley on her sea trials and can order her to fitout at sea."

"Do it! John, contact the English and get permission for a fighter wing to fly over for maneuvers out of a base there, but make it a night flight, Okay?"

"Yes, sir."

"Everybody else, stand down for now."

Joel M. Fulgham

1800 hrs USS Hunley Radio Room

"Chief, we have priority orders coming in over the DWRR."

"Okay, feed it through the decoder. I'll alert the conn." The chief picked up the sound powered phone and growled the conn. "Officer of the Deck, this is radio. Priority orders coming in. Looks like you need to inform the Captain."

"Will do, Chief. Messenger, tell the Captain priority orders are coming in. She's probably in the wardroom."

"Aye, aye, sir."

Helen and most of the Officers were finishing their meals. "Excuse me, Captain. The Officer of the Deck requested I inform you that we have urgent orders coming through."

"Very well, seaman. Tell the Officer of the Deck the XO will pick them up from radio." She turned to James, "James, kindly pick them up and bring them to my cabin."

"Yes Ma'am, right away. If you will excuse me." The XO stood and headed for the radio room.

"I'll fill the rest of you and the crew in as soon as I know what's happening. Now, if you will all excuse me." The other officers stood up as the Captain left the room.

A few minutes, later James arrived at the Helen's cabin, "Captain, I have the orders."

"Good. Come in and please have a seat." She took the envelope, opened it and removed the contents. She read the paper quickly then looked up at James, "It looks like we're not going to Andros. We are to make best speed, while maintaining radio contact, to a point 50 miles west of the Virgin Islands and meet up with the USS Frank Cable for a final fitout and load live torpedoes. We will also receive new orders there. Since they want us to maintain radio contact, we will be limited to 50 knots. The way I see it, we should be able to rendezvous about 0800 tomorrow. What do you think?"

"I think that's a close guess, Captain, but after I see the charts, I'll be more certain. I'll have the Navigator plot the course. But you know, these orders don't make sense. Why would they send a boat that hasn't finished sea trials to resupply at sea? What do you think is going on?"

"I don't have a clue and it looks like no one else does, either. I'll inform the crew in a few minutes. Have the Navigator plot the new coarse, but don't tell him why. Here's the list of what we'll need from the Cable. Once you know when we'll reach the Cable, have radio send our list and ETA to them."

"Aye, Aye, Ma'am."

For several minutes after James left, Helen sat looking at the wall, her features slightly twisted in concentration. Finally, she took a deep breath, stood and headed for the conn. "Captain, I've reviewed the charts with the Navigator and at 50 knots, we'll be at the area of the Cable at 0900 tomorrow. I was about to have radio send the message."

"Okay, thanks. Navigator, do you have the new heading?"

"Yes, Ma'am, 175 degrees."

"Good. Officer of the Deck, bring us to a new heading of 175 degrees, make speed ahead full, and have all off-watch personnel muster on the mess deck."

Ten minutes later, the crew was packed into the mess deck when the Captain entered. "Someone turn on the PA system." She spoke into the mike, "Fellow officers and crew. We will not be going to the test range for practice. Instead we'll have to offload our practice torpedoes and bring on war shots. We'll also have to make whatever repairs are needed while tied up to the Cable at sea. I want everything accomplished in three days. That may require working around the clock, so I want division officers to check their worklists and prepare a schedule to accomplish this task. Division Officers, if you don't think this is possible, please let me know, but you better have a damned good reason. I'll be as honest as I can with you. Something doesn't add up. We haven't tested our fire control system, so we don't even know that it will work correctly. So, make of it what you will. We'll tie up to the Cable at about 0930 tomorrow so let's get a good night's rest and be ready to go asses and elbows in the morning. Thank you for your support and hard work." With that the Captain left and the crew slowly filed out and turned into their racks.

Chapter 5

0845 "Captain to the Conn," came over the intercom.

"Captain we have a surface contact at 10,000 yards, bearing three-five-one degrees relative, speed zero."

"Very well. Officer of the Deck, take us up to periscope depth. It should be the Cable. Once the contact is verified, surface and request permission to come alongside."

"Yes Ma'am. Diving Officer, take us to periscope depth."

"Periscope depth, aye, sir. Ten degrees rise on the dive planes, ahead 1/3 sir. Flood negative. Passing two hundred feet, Sir. Passing one hundred feet. Decrease dive planes to two degrees. Very well, zero your planes, maintain depth sixty feet. We are at Periscope depth, sir."

"Very well. Raising scope number two." As soon as the periscope broke the water the Officer spun in a circle to check for other vessels in the vicinity. Once satisfied there where no other ships around, he returned to the contact sonar had reported. It was a small shape in the distance at first, but switching to a higher magnification, he identified the submarine tender. After several minutes, he could make out the hull number AS-40. "That's the Cable. Prepare to surface." The Diving Officer issued a series of orders and the announcement was made, "Surface, surface, surface. All ahead, standard."

Once on the surface the Officer of the Deck moved to the bridge with two lookouts and a signalman. "Signalman, contact the Cable and request permission to come alongside."

"Aye, aye." The signalman flashed the Officer's request. Several minutes later came the response, "Permission granted. Come along the port side."

"Thank you Petty Officer." Leaning down to the intercom and pressing the switch, "Diving Officer, blow maneuvering tanks."

"Blow maneuvering tanks, Aye, Sir," came back over the speaker. As the tanks were emptied the hull rose and raised the bridge.

With the hull awash, the Officer of the Deck called to the control room. "Ring up ahead full." As the Hunley passed the starboard side of the Cable at approximately five hundred yards, "Slow to 1/3. Station the line handlers." Within seconds crewmembers opened the main hatch and scrambled topside. The Officer of the Deck kept an eye on the ship and when he felt there was enough room; he ordered the helm left fifteen degrees and the sub swung around slowly. The turn took the sub in a wide u around the ship and brought her to a position aft. "Zero your rudder, reduce speed to five knots."

The sub came alongside, the Cable and stopped. Mooring lines were thrown from the tender and the sub tied up. As the ladder was lowered from the Cable, Helen came out the aft hatch and waited for the ladder to be secured, then hurried up it to report to the Submarine Squadron Commodore.

Later, when she returned to the sub and went to her cabin, Bill had finished packing his things in preparation for leaving the boat.

"Bill, it's been a pleasure having you aboard and I appreciate all you've done."

"Think nothing of it, Helen. You just take good care of her and she'll always bring you home."

"I'll remember that. You take care of yourself. And by the way, she's a nice boat."

"Thanks. I'll be seeing you around." Bill picked up his gear and left.

Day two of fit out. 0913

Over the boat's announcing system, "Captain to the Radio room."

A few minutes later, Helen entered the Radio room, "Yes, Chief, you need me?"

"Captain, we just received a flash message," the radio chief replied with a sad look in his eyes.

"Well, what is it?"

"Ma'am, the message is a gray lady down. There's been no contact with the USS Green Bay for the last two days. All vessels in the Mediterranean are ordered to a search for her off the west coast of Sicily."

Helen froze briefly before plopping down into a chair while trying to gather herself. "That doesn't make any sense. Captain Angst is a good seaman. He wouldn't just lose his boat in the middle of the Med. Something's going on that's not being revealed. All we can do for now is pray that she turns up somewhere. Chief, hand me the mike. 'Attention all hands; this is the Captain. We just received a gray lady down message. The USS Green Bay has not been heard from in two days and is presumed down somewhere off the coast of Sicily. A search for it is now underway. I know all our prayers go out to her crew that they'll be found safe. As soon as we receive further word I'll pass it on to you.' Thank you, Chief. Let me know as soon as you hear anything else."

"Yes Ma'am. By the way, Captain, I served with Captain Angst on the Los Angeles. If you want to talk about it, I already know what happened between you two and how you must feel now."

"Thanks, Chief, I'll be alright."

A few seconds later in the XO's stateroom.

"Jim, I'm going to see the Commodore and try to find out what Matt was up to. I can't imagine him losing his boat in the middle of the Med. It just doesn't make any sense. If any more information comes over the radio, send a messenger for me."

"Aye, aye, Ma'am. Did you know Captain Angst?"

"Excuse me Jim, but that question should be, do I know him," her voice sounded irritated for the second time that Thomas could ever remember.

"Sorry."

"An honest slip. Sorry I over-reacted. To answer your question, yes, we go way back. I'll be with the Commodore if you need me." With that she hurried off the sub.

When she reached the Commander's stateroom, she paused for a moment to catch her breath and straighten her uniform before knocking. "Enter."

"Commodore, can I have a word with you?" She slowly entered the large room that served as an office, meeting room and lounge. To one side was a small area that served as a bedroom.

"Hello, Helen. Sure, come on in. I've been expecting you ever since I heard about Matt's boat. You want something to drink?"

"No thanks, Commodore. What I would like to know is what's going on. Matt wouldn't lose a boat like this."

"You're right." The Commodore took a deep breath before continuing. "Helen, when you received orders to meet us here, Matt was ordered to investigate a group of transport vessels off the Libyan coast. We haven't heard from him, so we assume something went wrong and they were unable to send a message."

"Why are you searching off Sicily?"

"Matt was surely inside Libya's territorial waters, so we can't search there, can we? And we have to search somewhere, for political reasons and to satisfy family members."

"You're right, Commodore, I'm just not thinking clearly. So what's the Republic up to anyway?"

"Don't know. We're still in the dark about the whole thing. God, I wish we had at least one satellite up so we could see what size groups were moving around. It's been reported that the group in the Med has two carriers and two more coming up the west coast of Africa."

"Have we taken any measures to counter whatever they're up to?"

"No, the White House has ordered us to take no action that could be interpreted as hostile. However, since you brought it up, would you recommend Mr. Thomas for command?"

"Yes, without any hesitation. But what do you mean, since I brought it up?"

"We are quietly bringing back some recently retired subs, and I want him to take command of the first one out."

"But Sir, we're scheduled to depart in two days. What are we supposed to do for an Executive Officer?"

"I have the perfect XO for you. He'll report aboard first thing tomorrow. And trust me, He'll be fine."

"Well, if you say so Commodore, but I'd prefer to know something about him before he comes aboard."

"I said, don't worry Helen. You already know him. Now, go back to your boat and make sure you're ready to shove off by tomorrow night."

"Tomorrow night! That'll be tight, Sir"

"I know your crew will be ready. I have faith in them and in you. Now, go."

"Aye, aye sir." Helen turned and left. The Commodore watched her and drew a heavy breath as she closed the door. He looked like a middle-aged, James Earl Jones, standing there looking at the closed door and worrying about how Helen would handle the news about Matt. He had met Helen at officers training school when she first entered the Navy and was instantly charmed by her. He became a mentor and friend to her while she was there. He watched her mature into one of the Navy's best officers and was proud of the role he had in her development. He was also the first to recommend her as Commanding Officer of the Hunley and sure she wouldn't let him down.

Once back on the boat, Helen went to the XO's cabin. "Jim, I have some good news for you. The Commodore asked me if I would recommend you for command and I did. You are being given your own boat. It's an old boat that's being reactivated, but at least it'll be yours."

"That's great. Thanks for the recommendation, but I don't want to leave you in a bind."

"Don't sweat it. The Commodore assures me that he has a capable replacement. Now get packed and get off my boat. And now call me Helen, Captain."

"Thanks again, Helen."

"Give it a few months and then we'll see if you still thank me." She turned and left.

Pentagon, Joint Chiefs of Staff

"Gentlemen, we now have a report from the USS Nashville regarding the carrier group heading north along the African coast. It consists of four carriers, eight cruisers, nine destroyers and frigates and possibly two subs."

"General, that's quite a force. The only reason for a force like that is war."

"Quite right, Admiral. Another part of the equation is that the search party in the Med reports the Republic has two more carriers groups heading west. With the transports at Libya, they may be preparing to attack either Morocco or Spain. That's my guess. Anyone have a different idea?"

"Well General, if they are really planning on going to war, I think they will attack both Morocco and Spain to control access to the Med. That would also trap our Ships there so they could eliminate them at their leisure. Do we have time to withdraw our ships from the Med?"

"No. The carrier group is already west of our ships. If it's really the start of a war, our ships are trapped, a lost cause. How many are in there?"

"Twenty five destroyers and frigates. Our only sub has already been lost."

"Speaking of subs, Admiral, what about the Republic's subs off our East coast?"

"Don't know. We've had no contact with them. Maybe they have gone home."

"No way. If they're ready for a war, it's obviously well planned. I think we should give the President one more try so that we don't get caught completely off guard. If we begin to mobilize now, we can at least be prepped for a quick response." General Wish reached for the intercom, "Lieutenant, get me the President on the phone."

"Yes Sir," replied the shaky voice over the phone.

"Admiral, if we fail to get the President's permission for some kind of action and they're really going to start a war, we are already behind in the game. And if that happens, you know who's going to be the scapegoat, don't you."

The young man's voice came back over the intercom, "General, I have the President's personal secretary on the line."

"Thank you, Lieutenant." The General reached for the phone, "This is General Wish. I must speak to the President."

"General, I'm sorry, but the President is busy now. I'm supposed to inform you that the Islamic Republic has found the missing submarine. Their Ambassador reported that the remains of a United States submarine is in their coastal mine fields. And furthermore, if we stay out of their territorial waters, we can avoid unfortunate incidents of this nature. The President says that if you continue to disobey his orders, he wants your letter of resignation."

"I understand. There won't be any other problems," the General replied in a solemn voice and slowly hung up the phone. He turned to the others, exasperated. "Steve, the Green Bay has been found. It's on the bottom, off the Libyan coast. Apparently she ran into a minefield and was damaged. We've been warned to stand down. Any further actions and we will be forced to resign."

"Our hands are really tied now. Can we at least go in and check for survivors?"

"No. They said to stay out of their waters. I guess you'd better get your people started notifying the next of kin. Tell them she was lost at sea in deep water."

"Yes Sir. I'll also inform Submarine Squadron four."

Knocking at the door interrupted the two men. It opened and a junior officer popped his head in. "Excuse me sirs, but CNN is reporting that General Kadala will hold a news conference at 0900 Eastern time, tomorrow morning, about a United States submarine that entered a mine field in their waters."

"Thank you Ensign," replied the General. He waited for the Ensign to leave before he continued. "Well, we should have known they would make a big show of this. Steve, tell the families the truth and hurry before that press conference."

"Okay," Steve said as he stood up from his chair. "Our work will, from here on, not be easy. I suggest we call it a night. Tomorrow's shaping up to be a nightmare," He left the office.

On board the USS Frank Cable

A knock at the Commodore's stateroom door, "Enter."

"Commodore, we just received this message for you, top secret."

World War III
The Beginning

"Very well, bring it here Petty Officer Hass." The Petty Officer crossed the office and handed the envelope to the Commodore. "Thank you, that will be all." The Petty Office turned and left the office, closing the door behind him. The Commodore, opened the sealed envelope and read:

> Commodore, I regret to inform you that the Islamic Republic reports a United States submarine has been destroyed off the coast of Libya. There were no survivors. The Department of the Navy believes a navigational error caused the submarine to stray into the minefield. Please inform the personnel in your command.
>
> Admiral Steve Schmidt
> Chief of Naval Operations

"I guess I should go tell Helen first. Damn, I hate this part of the job," the Commodore thought.

A few minutes later, aboard the Hunley, the Commodore approached the Captain's open stateroom door. "Helen," she looked up from her desk.

"You must have bad news to come down here in person."

"I just received a message from the CNO. The Islamic Republic reports a US sub has been sunk in one of their coastal mine fields. There were no survivors."

"We'd suspected that much. What's the official version?"

"That the Captain became lost and sailed into their territorial waters. Whatever happened, it was totally his fault."

"That sounds just like what those chicken-shits in Washington would say. So what's our next step?"

"Nothing, for now. General Kadala is holding a press conference tomorrow. Until then, we have to wait and deal with the fallout from what he says."

"Anymore word on the Islamic fleet?"

"It looks like they'll rendezvous at the Straits of Gibraltar tomorrow afternoon. Other than that, we don't have a clue. Will you be ready to get underway tomorrow?"

"Yes, sir. You are aware aren't you, that we still haven't checked out the impulse drive?"

"Yes, I am, but your new Executive Officer will be capable of correcting any problems you may encounter with that drive system." He looked at his watch. "I must be getting back to the ship. I'll see you tomorrow before you leave. Good night, Helen."

"Good night, Commodore. Thanks for coming down."

He left and Helen sat there remembering the last time she had seen Matt. They were lying on a moonlit beach in the Caribbean and she blurted out, "Matt, make love to me."

"Your wish is my command." He rolled over, pulled her to him and began passionate kissing her as he expertly unfastened the top of her bikini. He rolled her onto her back as he tossed the top aside and kissed her neck. He slowly moved down to her small pert breasts, kissing each lovingly.

His hands progressed down to the strings of her bottom and gave a sharp tug that released the bow. Her hands reached inside the top of his trunks and pulled them off.

"Matt let's go in the water," Helen whispered into his ear. With a smile, he gently picked her up and carried her into the surf where their bodies mingled in passion.

Chapter 6

0900 ET CNN General Kadala address
"Three days ago, a United States submarine, sent to spy on our Naval training exercises within our territorial waters, entered one of our coastal mine fields and exploded. We, the people of the Islamic Republic, have had enough United States interference in our affairs and now proclaim that we will no longer permit these intrusions into our waters and air space. As I address you, our forces are reclaiming our ancestral land of Palestine. Furthermore, to ensure that the United States can no longer interfere with our sovereign rights, our military forces are taking control of Morocco and Spain. This will ensure the United States military will no longer pollute the waters of the Mediterranean Sea with their presence."

"All United States ships currently in the Mediterranean Sea are hereby ordered to surrender or be destroyed. Any aggressive acts by them will be considered an act of war between the United States and the Islamic Republic. A war the United States cannot win. We have a five to one advantage in ships and planes and ten-to-one in total fighting forces."

"We want only to protect our territory and the United States of America has demonstrated their reluctance to leave us alone. But now we can protect ourselves from the continued United States invasions of our territories and are willing to demonstrate our power and influence, to ensure our rights as a free civilization. The United States ships have 24 hours to comply with our order. Any Mediterranean Country that renders aid to the US ships will be punished in a most decisive manner."

The Pentagon
"Well, General looks like we were right. Now what action do we take?"

"Steve, the President may ask for my resignation, since Kadala claimed the sub provoked them to action. You and I know this was already in the works, but what that chicken in the White House will do is the question."

"Mike, call the President."

"Yeah, might as well get it over."

There is a knock at the door, "Excuse me, General, the President is on line for you."

"Well, that was quick. He must want to get the first punch in. Well, here goes my career." Mike said as he reached for the phone. "Yes Sir, Mr. President…Yes Sir, I did see General Kadala's press conference…Yes Sir. We will be there in one hour."

Mike hung up and took a deep breath, "Well, looks like we're still in business. The President wants a meeting with us in one hour. We're also ordered to prepare all satellites for launch." Reaching for the intercom, "Sergeant, have all senior officers and intelligence people in the command room, now. And get two helos warming up on the pad. It's time to go to work."

"Attention!" Announced the Private as the General and Admiral entered the command room.

"Carry on," the General replied as he walked to his chair at the head of the table. "Ladies and Gentleman, we have a serious situation before us. As you already know the, Islamic Republic has declared war on us. The President wants to meet with us in approximately one hour and then we should know what our response will be. Meanwhile, we have to learn what our war status is and determine what we are capable of immediately responding with. The President has already ordered the preparation of our satellites for launch. General, what's the status on them?"

"Once you issue the order, they'll be in orbit and operational inside of two hours."

"Excuse me, General." A Sergeant appears at the door.

"Yes, Sergeant."

"We're receiving information from our embassy in Jerusalem. They are under heavy bombardment from both aircraft and artillery units. It is unconfirmed, but it appears the Israeli Air Force has been wiped out. Reports are that the Islamic ground forces are moving rapidly toward the city. That's the end of the report."

"Thank you, Sergeant. Have we heard from Spain or Morocco?"

"No, Sir."

"General, what about our ships still in the Med?"

"Good question, any suggestions?"

"Yes, Mike. We could use the Hunley to attack their ships and lure them away from Gibraltar enough to allow our ships to sneak out. If they can't sneak out, maybe they could at least fight their way out."

"How long will it take to bring carriers near enough to aid the attack, maybe even the odds a bit?"

"We can have the Reagan in range by tonight. If you want two carriers, it'll take three days. The Hunley will take two days to get there, anyway. If you want to even the odds more, we can move some Air Force squadrons nearer to assist in the attack."

"Fine, we'll keep that in mind. But, how can the Reagan be in range by tonight?"

"That's right, you don't know do you? I had her move to the West coast of England after our meeting with the President."

"You took that on yourself after we were told not to? What balls!"

"Mike, the President said he didn't want any action that could be misunderstood. The group moved there at normal cruising speed."

"Okay Steve, I got your point. Robert, how long before we can get ground troops to Europe?"

"We can begin airlifts tonight or tomorrow."

"We can also board troops on transport ships and put to sea late tomorrow."

"Thanks, Bob. John, What about air strikes?"

"Give the word and we'll be airborne within fifteen minutes."

"Any other Intelligence to report?"

"No Sir."

"Okay then, let's head over to the White House, the Helos are on the pad."

10:30 the Situation Room at the White House.

"Well General, your sub played right into Kadala's hands, didn't it. Without that, there wouldn't be any question of right or wrong. The only reason you're still here is because, damn it, you were right. Now, that's all I have to say about that. What to do now is the question. The U.N. is convening at this time to try and persuade

Kadala to retreat. However, that's unlikely, since this is an obviously well-planned operation. Since we do not want to give Kadala a reason to escalate the hostilities until the U.N. has failed, all plans made now will be contingency and await further orders. Is that understood, General?"

"Yes, Sir."

"Jenny Watson, our Secretary of State, will update you on what we know"

She speaks, "We are getting a pretty good picture of what we're up against. Israel has been hit hard and considered lost. Morocco will be completely under the Republics control by tomorrow. In Spain, a line that runs twenty miles south of Madrid to Gibraltar, has been occupied, by an estimated some 200,000 men. If Kadala wants to, he has sufficient men to completely occupy all of Spain."

"Madam Secretary, how could they have landed 200,000 men in such a short time?"

"It appears that 100,000 were brought in by sea. Airlifts have also been running constantly since nine this morning and it is believed that some 20,000 were already in Spain before this started. Are there any other questions concerning the invasion forces? Okay. English and French pilots have been flying recon and report five enemy carriers in the Atlantic and two in the Med, plus their support craft and screens. Several other enemy fighter and bomber squadrons have been flying out of airports in southern Spain. So you see, this attack was well planned and executed, with little resistance. Spain has grouped its forces around Madrid, to defend further advance. But as we know, they don't have much of a military."

"Sounds like the Republic brought in enough men to thwart any counter-attack. What are your plans to get our ships out of the Med?" ask an Admiral.

"Admiral, we are currently using diplomatic channels to get Kadala to let them go. In the meantime, you should come up with a plan."

"We already have one, Ma'am, and I promise we'll not make it easy for the Republic. If we don't get the ships out, we'll, at least, take out a chunk of their fleet."

"Excuse me, Admiral. How long will it take to put your plan into action?" The President finally spoke.

"Three days, Mr. President. That is, once you give the word."

"That's two days more than Kadala gave us."

"Yes Sir, but maybe your diplomatic efforts can buy us the time we need. Besides, sir, if you would have let us take action when we first requested it, our response time would now be considerably less."

"General, I can make you the goat in this, but that won't do our troops any good, will it?" Mike stared at the President and shook his head, no. "Have you heard the Admiral's plan and do you agree with it?"

"Yes, Sir. It'll take everything we can move into the area, though. If it works, it'll weaken their navy and maybe buy us time to get our military up to speed. That is, if you and Congress let us."

After a long, thoughtful pause, the President decided. "Okay, so far, the Republic has only threatened action against us. Therefore, we will not engage them at this time. However, we will ready our forces for an immediate retaliation against any further aggressive action. The English have given us permission to operate from their airbases, so General, I suggest you deploy the F-122Bs, as well as your fighter force, just in case. I'll back any other deployments you deem necessary, with the exception of ground forces. I do request however, that you mask the deployment, if possible. I'll also take up your money request with the congressional leadership. Now, I'd like to know how you're planning to defend the fleet that's currently in the Med?"

"We're having them group north of Corsica. There we'll be able to provide air cover from England or better yet, if you can arrange it, from France."

"I understand, General." The President turned to Jenny, "Contact the French ambassador and work out the details for our planes to operate from there?"

"Yes, sir, Mr. President."

"If that's all, we have work to do. Gentleman. If you will excuse us?" The President left the room with Jenny close behind.

Joel M. Fulgham

A few minutes later in the helicopter headed for the pentagon.

"Steve, when we get back, have the Bush and Hunley link up with the Reagan. Also, have as many ships as possible get underway and take up defensive positions from Greenland to the Bahamas. And do whatever you can in the Pacific. We know they have a few carriers out there. John, send two more fighter squadrons, both F-122B squadrons and another bomber squadron to England. Bob, the Army and Marines are now on standby. I want to be able to deploy with only an hour's notice."

USS Cable

"Commodore, you wanted to see me?"

"Yes, Helen, come in. I want you to meet your new Executive Officer, Lt. Commander William Floyd."

"Hi, Helen. I bet you didn't expect to see me so soon."

"When did you join the Navy?"

"About twenty years ago. For the past ten, I've been on inactive reserve. Now, do you have a problem with me being your new XO?"

"No, not at all. At least you already know the boat. Welcome aboard."

The Commodore spoke up. "Excuse me, I hate to interrupt, but we have other business to discuss. So please have a seat. I'm sure you both heard what happened this morning. What you don't know is we're planning a counter attack and you will be the spearhead. You're to hook up with the Reagan, off the west coast of England and wait. Then you'll coordinate with the Reagan and Bush battle groups to engage a Republic fleet of at least five carriers. With your speed and new weapons, we hope that you can take out or disable at least two carriers before they know what's happening. Then making noise, you're to lure some of their ships from the area. If it gets too hot, though, put some distance between you and them. The main purpose of this attack is to get our ships out of the Med, so do what you can to help them."

"Yes, Sir. Commodore, can we to test the impulse drive on the way?"

"That depends on when you're ready to sail."

"We'll be ready, once we're finished loading the torpedoes. Probably this afternoon."

"Then you should have time. It'll take the Bush three days to link up with you. Good luck and good hunting."

"Thank you Sir. Have more fish ready for us when we get back, we'll need a new load." Helen and Bill left the stateroom together, "Welcome back, Bill. It's nice to know that your life now also depends on how well you designed the Hunley."

Bill smiled at her and replied, "If I would have known I'd be going into battle with her, I would have tightened all the bolts a bit more. You know, this has to be the first time a boat designer sees his creation in action."

"You're probably right. Now, which bolts need tightening?" The two laughed as they walked down the ladder to the Hunley.

1800 hours

As Helen sat in deep concentration, looking over a pile of charts on her desk, she was startled by a knock at her door, "Excuse me, Captain. We're loading the last torpedo and we'll be ready to get underway by 2000 hours."

"Thank you Lieutenant. The crew has done an excellent job of swapping the torpedoes. Please thank them for a job well done."

"Yes, Ma'am." The Weapons Officer replied as he turned and left, smiling an approval for himself.

In her cabin, Helen picked up the phone. "Control room, this is the Captain."

Instantly came the answer, "Aye, Captain, this is the Officer Of the Deck."

"Make necessary preparations to get underway at 2000 hours."

"Yes, Ma'am. We'll be ready," replied the slightly-excited voice. Helen hung the phone up and went back to studying her charts.

2000 hours

Lieutenant Gorecki was on to the bridge in preparation of getting the boat underway. The intercom came to life, "Bridge, Control Room. All stations manned and ready to get underway. Maneuvering reports ready to answer all bells."

Joel M. Fulgham

He pressed the speaker switch, "Very well, standby." Releasing the switch he took a long look around the topside of the boat and up at the massive ship to which they were tied. Drawing a deep breath he called out to the line handlers, "Single up all lines!"

The men and women at the four cleats that each held three strands of rope sprang into action and tossed all but one line off each. The Chief Petty Officer in charge yelled back, "All lines are singled!"

"Very well, cast off lines two and three!" The two groups behind the sail removed the remaining lines and tossed the ends over the side with a splash. "Lines two and three clear!" yelled the Chief.

"Cast off line one!" The group at the bow removed their line from the cleat and tossed it over the side. With the line removed the bow started to drift away from the tender. "Cast off line four!" That completed, he pressed the intercom switch and spoke into it, "Five degrees starboard, ahead slow," then looked down at the deck, "Chief, clear the deck!"

"Aye, Aye Sir. All hands lay below." As the boat continued to pull away from the tender the line handlers scrambled down the deck hatches. The last one closed the outer hatch, continued down and closed the inner hatch and spun the hand wheel shut. He picked up the phone by the ladder, "Control Room, Machinery Room. The aft hatch is shut and dogged."

The Control Room phone talker checked the hatch indication then replied, "Confirmed. We indicate green." Lowering her mouthpiece, "Diving Officer, the Machinery Room hatch is shut." The sequence of reports and checks was repeated for the forward deck hatch.

"Very well." The Dive reached for the intercom, "Bridge, Control Room. We're ready to flood the maneuvering tanks."

Back on the bridge, Gorecki took a quick look around to satisfy himself they were clear of the tender, then spoke into the intercom, "Flood maneuvering tanks. Ahead two thirds."

"Flood the maneuvering tanks, ahead two thirds, aye." The long hull of the boat slowly sank below the surface. In a matter of seconds all that remained above the water was the sail. When the sub was well away from the tender, Gorecki ordered the lookouts to clear the bridge. Once they were below, he closed the cover on the intercom and followed them down, closing the hatches as he descended. Once the bottom hatch was dogged shut, he ordered, "Dive the boat."

The Diving Officer picked up the mike for the announcing system and called out, "Dive, Dive, Dive," then hit the diving alarm.

"We have green across the board," chimed in the Chief of the Watch.

"Open all main ballast tank vents, five degree down bubble. Make your depth 150 feet," continued the Diving Officer.

"Quartermaster, give me a heading."

"Sir, the heading should be zero-niner-five."

"Very well, Quartermaster. Dive, bring us to port, to new heading of zero-niner-five, all ahead standard."

Chapter 7

The next morning at the Pentagon

Mike Wish is talking on the phone. "Good morning, Steve. We've finally received word from the White House. France has offered us use of their airbases. And, that's not the best news. France has even offered the Bonaparte to support our counter attack. England has offered both the Sir Galahad and Sir Lancelot."

"What brought this on, Mike?"

"You haven't heard? The Republic has attacked Madrid and I guess the European countries are getting scared. Moreover, France has even allowed us to move ground forces onto their territory. Now, do you have any status on the Med fleet?"

"Most of the ships have grouped, but a few stragglers are still trying to make it to the rendezvous. I also understand the air cover is in place, but reporting no contact with hostile forces."

There's a knock at Mike's door. "Excuse me Steve, there's someone at the door." Steve presses the hold button, calls out, "Enter."

An officer enters. "Excuse me General, the John Rogers is reporting they've been engaged by hostile forces."

"Inform combat center I'm on my way." He speaks rapidly into the phone, "Steve, better get to the combat center, they have radio contact with the John Rogers! She's under attack! I'll meet you there in a few minutes?"

"I'm on my way." Mike hangs his phone up then looks at the map on the wall before heading out of his office.

Combat Center

"Attention on Deck."

Steve enters "Carry on. Captain, what do you have?"

"Admiral, it appears the Rogers is currently under heavy air attack. We've heard comments of three splashes. But, she has apparently taken several direct hits and is burning."

"Can we get her air support?"

World War III
The Beginning

"No, Sir. She's just rounded the southern tip of Greece. We've ordered the two nearest ships to double back and give aid, but unfortunately they're still an hour away. All we can hope to do is recover survivors."

The radio came alive. "This is the USS John Rogers, Mayday, mayday! We are abandoning ship. Our position is 200 miles southwest of Kalamai, Greece."

"Attention on Deck."

Mike enters, "As you were. Steve, what's happening?"

"The Rogers' crew is abandoning ship. There are two of our ships en route to her and they'll be there in about an hour."

"Where were they sunk?"

"Two hundred miles southeast of Greece."

"Have the other ships make best speed to Corsica. The Rogers' crew will have to make it to Greece on their own."

"Mike, you can't be serious. Those people are expecting help and will stay in the area waiting for it."

"When help doesn't arrive they'll figure it out and head for land. Did the Rogers give any indication of where the planes were from?"

"Yes Sir, Tripoli."

"Thank you, Lieutenant. Steve, meet me in my office in one hour. I'm going to inform the President."

"Right."

One hour later.

"Mike I'm sorry about the little misunderstanding in the Com Center. I realize why you ordered the ships to turn around."

"Well, don't do it again. You're my right hand and we mustn't show a divided front right now. I spoke to the President and he's going to release the story about the Rogers and call a meeting with Congressional leaders. In the meantime, I requested permission to strike at Tripoli and he agreed. We have a meeting in a few minutes, but immediately afterwards make arrangements for two more carriers to come out of mothballs. The Saratoga and her crew are already being activated from the Naval Academy. You have any idea how long it'll take to get her ready?"

"If the middies have kept her shipshape, we could scrape a crew together in two or three weeks. Then another two weeks to fit her out and another week or two for a shakedown. I'd guess a month-and-a-half to two months."

"Tell you what, Steve, You have one month to get her headed to wherever the battles are by then. Okay, now let's go see the others."

"If you were only going to give me a month, why'd you ask?"

"Being polite. Let's go."

Meeting of the Joint Chiefs of Staff.

"Gentleman we've been given permission to conduct an air strike against Tripoli to avenge the sinking of the Rogers. It'll be a limited strike and, it's set for tonight at 2100 hours, French local time. The F-122B squadron will strike military bases in the Tripoli area. Once they've destroyed their targets they'll return to base and no further action will be taken. Now, on to the major operations. By order of the President, we're directed to call up all reserve units, both active and inactive and make preparations for their deployment."

"General Freeman, bring back those fighter wings you spoke of the other day. Also have personnel work around the clock to get as many of the C-141 Starlifters operational as you can. However, we still do not have permission to launch the satellites."

"If there aren't any questions let's get on it, the Republic already has a couple of years jump on us."

USS Hunley

The Officer of the Deck spoke into a microphone. "Maneuvering, Conn, prepare to shift propulsion to the impulse drive units."

"Conn, Maneuvering, Prepare to shift propulsion to impulse drive, aye."

The Engineering Officer of the Watch switched to the engine room announcing system. "Engineering Watch Supervisor, prepare to shift propulsion to impulse drive."

The Engineering Watch Supervisor then moved to the seawater valve operating station to meet the Engine Room Supervisor.

"Okay Parker, open port and starboard impulse drive suction and discharge valves."

"Open impulse drive suction and discharge valves, aye, Chief." The man operated the valve control levers and the two watched as the red indicator light went out. A few seconds later, the green indicator light came on. "Valves indicate open, Chief."

"Very well. Now shut the electrical breakers for the pump motors."

"Shut the power breakers, aye." The young Petty Officer headed forward to an electrical panel and unscrewed the splashguard, shut the breakers and replaced the covers. "Breakers are shut, Chief."

"Very well, I'll inform Maneuvering." The chief stepped to the curtain in the doorway of the maneuvering area and pushed them aside. "Request permission to enter."

"Enter Chief."

"Sir, the engine room is ready to shift propulsion."

"Very well, Chief. Throttleman, test the pumps."

"Test the pumps. Aye, Sir." The throttleman turned two small handwheels until there was a slight deflection on the impulse drive pressure gauges. "Pumps tested sat, Sir."

"Very well." He then switched back to the intercom. "Conn, Maneuvering. We're ready to shift propulsion."

After a brief pause, "Maneuvering, Conn. Shift propulsion to impulse drive."

"Conn, Maneuvering. Shift to impulse drive, aye. Throttleman, all stop. Disengage magnetic drive system."

"Answering all stop." The throttleman reached up and turned a switch, "Magnetic drive disengaged, sir."

"Very well. Throttleman, answer all-ahead one-third on the impulse drive."

"All ahead one-third, aye." The throttleman then turned the hand wheels again until the proper pump pressures were reached. "Answering ahead one-third on port and starboard impulse drive units."

"Very well."

"Conn, Maneuvering. Impulse drive engaged, answering ahead one-third."

At the Conn. "Very well. Dive, mark speed, then ring up ahead two-thirds."

"Speed is twelve knots, ringing up two-thirds. Maneuvering answering two-thirds."

"Very well. When speed stabilizes, mark it."

"Speed is twenty knots."

"Very Well. Ring up ahead standard and mark."

"Ahead standard, aye." After a few minutes, "Thirty knots, sir."

"Excellent. Ring up ahead full and mark."

"Ahead full, aye." After a few minutes, "thirty-eight knots, sir."

"Messenger, inform the Captain we are answering ahead full, speed thirty-eights knots. Request permission to go to a flank."

"Yes, Sir." Replied the seaman and headed forward. In a few minutes the messenger returned. "Officer of the Deck, Captain said to standby."

"Come in," Bill answered a knock at his door as he lay on his bunk. The door slowly opened and Helen stuck her head in. "Oh, Helen, I mean Captain, excuse me."

"Gone to bed already Bill, it's only 2100."

"Just relaxing while refreshing my memory on battle tactics."

"You should know better than to lie down while reading that stuff. You'll fall asleep."

"Yes, ma'am."

"Besides, it'll all come back when we're in the thick of it. We might even rewrite the book with the Hunley. I stopped by because we're ready to go to flank on the impulse drive unit and it's time for you to take charge. I want you to relieve the Officer of the Deck and take us to flank speed. This crew thinks of you as an engineer, but you have to show them you are also a commander."

"Yes, Ma'am. I'll be right there."

A few minutes later on the Conn. "Lieutenant, I'm relieving you as Officer of the Deck."

"Are you sure, XO?"

"Yes, I'm sure. Do you have a problem with that?"

"No, not at all, sir."

After a detailed discussion of the status of the boat Bill, finally relieved the Lieutenant and ordered up ahead, flank.

"Officer of the Deck, Answering ahead flank. Ship's speed, forty-nine knots."

"Very well." Bill picked up the intercom mike, "Maneuvering, this is the XO. Have all stations take full set of readings and bring a copy to my cabin when you are relieved."

The calm of normal everyday routine was suddenly shattered by the sound of the collision alarm. After a few seconds of no follow-up report, Bill picked up the mike again. "Station sounding collision alarm, report!" After no response Bill ordered all hands to check for the collision alarm source.

"Officer of the Deck. We're losing depth control!"

"Chief of the Watch, commence pumping ballast overboard from the depth control tanks. Dive, emergency rise on the planes! Ahead standard. Messenger, man the sound-powered phones!"

Finally, a report came over the announcing system. "Flooding in the main pump room!"

Bill clicked the mike, "Maneuvering, shut port and starboard impulse drive valves. Shift propulsion to magnetic drive. Damage Control Party, muster in the crews' lounge."

"Officer of the Deck, the scene reports flooding has stopped."

"Very well. Dive, ring up ahead two-thirds and maintain current depth."

"Ahead two-thirds, maintain current depth, aye."

"Chief, continue pumping as necessary to regain trim."

"Control Room, this is the scene, Petty Officer Johns is in charge at the scene. There's approximately four feet of water above the deck plates. Request you electrically isolate the main pump room before personnel enter. Also request to pump the water out of the main pump room."

Helen came into the control room, "Bill, what's going on?"

He held up a finger for her to wait, "Phone talker, have maneuvering electrically isolate the Main pump room and cross connect the trim and drain systems. Have the damage control party prepare to pump the water out, using the trim system."

He turned to Helen, "Captain, we had flooding in the main pump room. Shutting the impulse drive valves has stopped it, but the source is still unknown. Propulsion is back on magnet pulse drive and maneuvering is electrically isolating the pump room. We're preparing to remove the water."

"Officer of the Deck, Maneuvering reports the pump room has been electrically isolated. The scene reports they're ready to commence pumping."

"Phone talker. Inform maneuvering that we will pump it out with the trim system and drain pump. Have maneuvering shift control of the drain pump to the control room. Chief of the Watch, commence pumping the main pump room to the depth control tanks when you have control of the drain pump."

"Aye, sir."

"Phone talker, has there been any word from the person on watch in the pump room."

"I'll ask, Sir."

Helen was satisfied that Bill had things under control and spoke up, "Bill, looks like you have a handle on the situation. I'm going down to the pump room."

"Aye, aye, Captain."

"Officer of Deck, scene reports no sign of fireman Johnson."

Bill picked up the microphone, "Corpsman and stretcher bearers lay to the crews' lounge."

"Officer of the Deck, scene reports the Captain is at the scene and personnel are entering the main pump room."

Helen leans over the ladder down to the main pump room and yells. "Find Fireman Johnson first!"

"Yes, ma'am." Almost instantly, "We've found her. Send the corpsman down she's unconscious. Looks like the force of the flooding pinned her between piping. Lucky for us she was next to the collision alarm."

Another crewmen entered the room and announced, "Captain, we've found the source of the flooding. Looks like a seal failure on the starboard drive pump."

"How long to repair it?"

"At least two hours for the pump, but the water reached the motors, so they'll need to be cleaned up. The same with the trim pump."

"Do you have any idea how long that will take?"

"No, ma'am. We'll have to have the electricians check it out first."

"Also, Fireman Johnson has been freed, and it looks like she'll be alright. But she won't be moving too fast for awhile."

"Thank you Corpsman, keep me posted. Petty Officer Johns, inform the Officer of the Deck that I want to meet with him, the Engineer, M-Division and E-Division Officers as soon as they have an estimate for repairs. I'll be in my quarters."

"Yes, ma'am. Phone talker, relay the message to the conn."

On the Conn.

"Officer of the Deck, to rendezvous with the carriers on schedule, we need to increase speed to forty-nine knots."

"Thank you, Quartermaster. Dive, ring up ahead standard. Maneuvering, make speed forty-nine knots."

0120 Knock, knock. "Enter."

"Captain, sorry to wake you, but we're ready for the briefing."

"Alright, Bill. I'll be right in," Helen replied. As she rose onto her elbows, the sheet slipped down, revealing her bare breast. Bill hurriedly excused himself, saying they'd be waiting in the wardroom. On his way to the wardroom, Bill wondered if Helen realized what had happened.

Everyone rose as the Captain entered the wardroom. "Stay seated. Seaman, bring me a cup of coffee, please." Turning back to the others, she announced, "Okay, what do we have?"

"Captain, replacing the pump's mechanical seal is already underway and should be finished in two hours. The real problem is repairing the electric motors. Both are full of salt. If everything goes right and if we concentrate on one at a time, we can get partial impulse drive in about twelve hours and full in twenty-four. By everything going right I mean if the clean water flushes are successful the first time. The good news is that the trim pump didn't get too wet, thanks to the up angle we were in. It should be operational in a couple of hours."

"What about working on both drive pumps?"

"Then you're looking at about twenty four hours for any type of impulse drive. It can take even longer, depending on how effective we are in removing the salt from the motor windings."

"Okay look, we have to be ready for battle in about twenty-four hours. Let's work on both and maybe one can be cleaned up and ready for partial use."

"You have your work to do, so get with it. Bill, hang around for a minute." After the other officers had left, Helen looked at Bill, "I hope I didn't embarrass you in my stateroom. Unfortunately, with both sexes in such cramped quarters, things like that happen. You'll get used to it. But, the real reason I wanted you to stay is to tell you that you did an excellent job on conn. It should go a long way toward winning the confidence of the crew. And see, I told you it would all come back."

"Thank you, Ma'am. It was nothing but pure instinct."

The Oval Office

"I called this meeting to fill you in on happening in the Med. A few hours ago, the Republic attacked and sank our destroyer, John Rogers. In retaliation, I have authorized an air strike against military bases in Tripoli, to demonstrate that we will not cower to their threats. With luck, the attack on Tripoli will convince the Republic to halt their aggression before this becomes World War III."

"Mr. President, the Republic outnumbers us two-to-one in ships and four-to-one in planes. Not to mention the ground forces. What makes you think they will back down?"

"I really don't expect them to. That's why I said, with luck. Tell me, do you think we should ignore their sinking the Rogers?"

"No, sir, not ignore it. Just pursue it through the United Nations."

"Senator Farnsworth, Spain and Israel have both taken their cases to the UN which appealed to the Republic to withdraw from their territory. The Republic dismissed every motion. Most countries have placed economic sanctions against them and they haven't flinched. In fact, they solidified their hold in every invaded country. What more do you suggest we do? Kiss their asses?"

"Not that. But since you asked, Mr. President, I think we should save ourselves. Offer to surrender the ships in the Med, if they allow the return of the crews. Then, offer to stay out of the Med if they withdraw from the occupied countries."

"What do mean save ourselves, Senator?"

"I don't think we have a chance against a military the size of the Republic."

"Senator, correct me if I'm wrong, but weren't you always boasting that our military forces are superior to the rest of the world and therefore we don't need as large a military?"

"Yes, but I didn't think anyone would challenge us. Besides, we needed the money saved for more social programs."

"You lying bastard! After all the years I supported you, everything you did was just a bluff! Get the hell out of my office! And don't count on my support anymore!" After the Senator stormed out, the President looked at the remaining Senators and Congressmen, "Do any of you feel the same way?"

The men and women sitting in the office looked at each other for a few moments before the Speaker of the House, Congressmen Gibson, spoke up, "Mr. President I think I speak for all of us when I say we're behind you all the way."

Israeli Defense Force, Jerusalem

The activity in the command post was chaotic as reports of the onslaught poured in. The numbers of bombers overhead outnumbered the anti-air-missile batteries available for defense. Whenever the Israelis would activate the radar systems to fire, standoff fighters would launch anti-radar missiles.

During the opening days of the war, The Israeli air force lost half of its combat strength. Now they couldn't even put an entire squadron together. Now, their remaining defenses were being systematically eliminated.

The Republic controlled the skies over Israel and diverted more planes to support the rolling thunder of the ground assault. Israel's tanks and artillery have, so far, successfully held back the

Islamic troops, but with the increased aerial attacks, they couldn't last much longer.

"General Netanyahu, radar shows another wave heading for artillery unit ninety-six."

"And where are they?"

"They're dug in on the east side of the Mount of Olives, sir."

"Captain, contact ninety-six and have them take cover. Shut down our radar systems before they lock in on it."

The radar system was shut down just as an anti-radar missile was fired from a fighter. Having lost its target, the missile sped past the radar station and plowed into a high-rise apartment building and exploded, gutting the building. The upper stories rocked briefly before tumbling to the ground.

Netanyahu stood in the center of the room, staring blankly at the wall, trying to come up with away to fight back. In desperation he made up his mind. "Radio, have ninety-six inform us when they have visual contact. Fire control, we'll go active on all missile batteries and launch. Then we'll continue firing until they fire back. Then we'll shut down our systems. Contact the Triple A batteries on the Mount of Olives and have them concentrate their fire on the heavy bombers. Maybe we can, at least, hurt them."

The command center was deathly quiet waiting for the visual report. Suddenly the speakers came to life, "Command, this is ninety-six. We have a visual! They're coming in, low and hot!"

"This is it! Radio, order all batteries to go active and fire at will! Radar, go active on our system." The orders were carried out and everyone waited for the action to start.

In seconds the radar operator spoke up, "General I count eighteen missiles outbound!"

"Keep the reports coming!"

"General, Standoff fighters have launched missiles!"

"Shut down all radar stations! Shit, that was too quick!"

The radio operator passed the word to shutdown the systems and the radar operator shut his down.

"How many missiles did we get off?"

"I counted twenty-three, General," the radar operator responded.

World War III
The Beginning

"Radio, I want casualty reports as soon as they're available." With these words, General Netanyahu retired to his office at the side of main room.

Twenty minutes later, the radio operator knocked on his door, "General, we have the casualty reports." He walked across the room, handed the folded paper to the general, then turned and left.

The general took a deep breath before opening the paper.

<u>Missile Batteries</u>
5 destroyed
2 damaged, out of action
12 operational
<u>AAA batteries</u>
37destroyed
17 operational
<u>Artillery</u>
15 destroyed
12 damaged, out of action
26 operational
<u>Bombers hit</u>
15 shot down
3 hit and damaged

"Well, that'll just about finish us. The Republic will take Jerusalem tomorrow."

Chapter 8

Tripoli, Islamic Republic 0130.

A beautiful, warm, summer night and a few cars were on the roads. The majority of the city was fast asleep, including, General Kadala. He was suddenly roused from his sleep by a massive explosion. He leapt from his bed and ran to the window. Outside all appeared quiet. The night exploded with a blinding flash that caused him to stumble backwards. Seconds later, a shock wave shattered the window, showering the room with huge shards of glass. The General screamed in agony as some ripped into his body. A servant burst into the room, and found the General on the floor, bleeding from numerous cuts.

Then his servant rushed to his side and gently lifted his head. "General, can you walk? We must hurry to the bomb shelter. The rest of your family is there already."

"Yes, I can walk, help me up." As the servant helped the General up, he looked out the window to see anti-aircraft fire rising into the smoky, black sky. Stunned, he looked at the servant and uttered, "What's happening?"

The servant responded, "I don't know sir, but we must go!"

Supported by the servant, the General limped his way to safety, three floors below the palace.

As the General and his servant entered the shelter, the Minister of Defense ran to him shouting, "General, the Americans are attacking! But they did not show up on our radar."

"What damage did they do?"

"The main assault was concentrated on our airfield with a smaller attack on the army base."

The General demanded, "Where is my family?"

"Your wife, daughter and two of your sons are in the family quarters. I regret to inform you that Aakmed was found dead in his room."

"Those damned American fools! They shall pay for this! Inform our operatives in America to commence their missions." With

*World War III
The Beginning*

the order given, the General collapsed in grief, too weak from his injuries and loss of blood to reach the family quarters.

High above Tripoli on board the Squadron Leader's F-122B.
"This is Dead Eye. Mission accomplished. Let's go home."

0920 Reagan International Airport Air Traffic Control Tower.
"Lear jet, November 8311 Romeo, this is Washington International. You are veering off course. Turn right to heading 170." After a tense moment, the air controller repeated the message. Then the blip of the small luxury jet disappeared from the air traffic controller's radar screen. In a state of shock, the controller turned to his supervisor. "Sir, I've just lost contact with a plane in the vicinity of the Mall."

"You what!" exclaimed the supervisor.

"I was vectoring a Lear for landing and it veered off course and disappeared from the screen."

"Are you reporting the plane went down near the White House?"

"Yes sir. The last contact I had was they were making a normal approach. Then nothing. The pilot never mentioned any problems or requested assistance."

"Okay. I'll alert the authorities."

0923 Observation Room in the top of the Washington Monument.
"Daddy look at that plane, it looks like it's coming straight at us."

"I see it, son. It sure does look that way." After mere seconds, the man screamed, "It is coming this way! Come on, we're getting out of here!" The man picked up his son and ran. Just as they started down the stairs, the monument was rocked by an explosion that sprayed glass throughout the observation room.

Outside, the air was full of the burning debris caused by the explosive-laden jet as it crashed into the White House. The Mall instantly became a mass of frantic, stunned people attempting to avoid the fireball. Closer to what was formerly the White House, bodies were everywhere. Some of those still alive, writhed in agony from cuts, missing limbs and burned flesh. Within minutes, police and ambulances arrived to assist the injured, but were inundated by the hysteric mob.

Meanwhile in the pentagon combat room.

"Gentleman, our raid last night was a complete success. If the rest of this conflict goes this well, all our troops should be home inside of three months." The General was gloating as the room was racked by what felt like an earthquake. The lights went out until the emergency generators brought the lights back on. "What the hell was that?"

A shaky voice rang out, "General, I can't reestablish communications with anyone."

"Damn it! Sergeant, go up to the com center and tell them we've lost communications down here again and that they better get it back pronto or I'll have their heads."

"Yes Sir," replied the Sergeant. He turned to the Staff Sergeant beside him and whispered, "You'd think he'd be used to this by now." He turned and left. A few minutes passed and a visibly-shaken Sergeant returned. "General, I'm afraid it may be a while before we get communication back."

"What's the problem, Sergeant? Are they on coffee break again?"

"No, sir. No one's there. In fact there's nothing above two levels up. That shock we felt was an explosion that destroyed everything up there."

"What the hell is going on? Sergeant, take whomever you need and get some communications down here. Everybody, let's get topside and see what we can do." They made their way outside and stopped as they looked around in stunned disbelief. "What the hell hit this place?" Even the experienced General could not comprehend the destruction. "Captain White, take charge here. From the looks of things, communication won't be restored for a while, so I'm taking the Joint Chiefs to Andrews Airforce Base and set up a temporary command center there. Private, go find a phone and get Andrews on the line! Tell them I need two helicopters here, yesterday! Tell them we have a National Emergency and need them to set up a command station in one of their hangers, complete with communications and a satellite uplink. Now get going!"

Steve looked over his shoulder at the General and yelled, "Mike, look here! It's wreckage from a plane."

The General scurried through the smoldering debris to the tail section of the jet. "That's impossible. A plane crashing couldn't possibly have done all this."

"Look at the size of this crater!" General Walton shouted.

After struggling through more debris, Mike found himself standing on the edge of a massive hole at least thirty feet across and ten feet deep. Steve came up behind Mike. "Shit! If a plane caused this, it had to be loaded with mucho explosives. Kadala?"

"Absolutely! The maniac is pulling out all the stops."

"Well, while we're waiting for the helos, let's see if we can find anybody in this mess who needs help."

After several minutes of rummaging through the debris and finding only bodies or body parts, a voice rang out, "General, General!"

"Over here, Private."

"Sir, the helos are on the way. Andrews reported that the White House was hit by a jet."

"What about the President?" Steve stiffened in anticipation.

"Relax, he left for Camp David early this morning. We have to get word to our forces to go with operation, 'Release.' Corporal Smith, go below and get us charts for England and the Western Med. Also grab some ship markers. And bring up some radios."

"Yes sir." The Corporal looked around until he found one of his buddies, "Hey Beats, come with me."

Another soldier approached. "General, we found four people still alive, but if medical aid doesn't show up soon, they're goners."

"Don't count on them making it. The White House was hit, too. If it's anything like this, emergency personnel are probably all down there. Captain White, How many bodies so far?"

"About fifty that are recognizable. No telling how many more, when we total up all the pieces."

General Wish looked up at the incoming Helicopters as the Corporal returned. "Captain White, take over here. We'll leave one helo for you to get survivors out as best you can."

The corporal came running up. "General, here's what you asked for."

"Thank you, Corporal. Here, Johnny, use these radios to communicate with the helo. He can relay information to us at Andrews. Good Luck." The General then ran to board the helicopter. As they took off, the men in the helicopters surveyed the vast damage. "Damn him!" was all the General could mutter.

Once at Andrews, the General ordered, "Get the President on the line."

"We already have an open line to him. He's been waiting for you. Please follow me, General." The General was escorted into a nearby hanger and directed to an office to one side. "Just press line one, Sir."

"Thank you, Lieutenant. That will be all for now. Oh, have your mess hall send over some food and coffee."

"Yes, Sir." The Lieutenant excused himself.

Pressing the button for line one, "Mr. President, you there."

"Yes, Mike, what's the situation at your place?"

"We're setting up a temporary command center now. With luck, we can be fully operational in a couple of hours. Sir, it's now time for you to make some decisions. First, you must shut down Reagan International, and let me setup air defenses around Washington. Second, we need to launch the satellites. And third, may we now proceed with a full scale deployment?"

"Steve I'm way ahead of you. I had the FAA issue a no-fly order within one hundred miles of downtown Washington. I've also called an emergency session of Congress for 7:00 P.M. tonight, for an official declaration of war against the Republic. At that time, you may launch all satellites and commence full-scale deployment. You can also deploy air defenses around the city, which is a reasonable precaution. Everything ready for tonight?"

"Last report was that they'd be ready to go at 9:00 P.M. our time."

"Good. By that time we should have a formal declaration. Have the troops send them a loud and clear message from the American People."

"Yes sir, Mr. President."

1310 USS Hunley

"Excuse me Captain, I have an update on the impulse drive situation."

"Good, come on in Bill."

"We're installing the starboard side motor now and it should be back in operation by 1800 hours. The port motor is in worse shape though. It appears the short melted some of the insulation on the windings and will have to be replaced. The only chance we have to fix it is if a shop on one of the carriers can rewire it, or if another ship has a replacement pump."

"Okay, give me the motor specification and I'll have radio contact them. If any can help, we'll go to ahead flank to gain more time to load and get it rigged for sea. Is there anything else we need?"

"Not that I am aware of."

"Okay then, you and the crew working on the pumps need some time in the rack."

"Good idea. I'll keep only the people I need to finish. Thanks."

1520 Andrews Airforce base

"General, we have contact with the Reagan."

"Good, inform them what has happened here, then tell them the President has directed them to deliver a loud, clear message to General Kadala tonight. May the winds of war be with them tonight."

1600 USS Hunley

Bill's sleep was interrupted by a knock at his door. "Enter," he mumbled as he tried to focus his mind.

"It's time to wake up."

"Oh, Helen it's you, come in."

"We're about to pull alongside the Reagan. They believe they have a motor that'll work, so I want you to go aboard and inspect it while I meet with the Admiral. Apparently we're spearheading tonight's attack and I'll give you the details when I get back."

"Okay. I'll be topside in a few minutes." A few minutes later, Helen and Bill were taken up to the carrier by a lift basket and went their separate ways. A half-hour later Bill returned to the boat, empty handed. While waiting for Helen to return, he toured the boat again and checked that everything was ready for battle. The only space not ready was the mess deck, where they were still cleaning up from the evening meal. In another hour this space would be ready also.

He had noticed a change in the crew over the last few days. They had become more intense as they performed their normal routine checks on the equipment. Every minute detail was being done more precisely. Even the manner they addressed each other had become more courteous. People who could previously not get along, were now polite and friendly to one another.

Bill's thoughts were broken by the announcement, "XO to the Captain's cabin." He reached Helen's door where she was waiting for him.

"Any luck?"

"No. The pumps they had couldn't fit down the hatch."

"Then we'll have to make do with what we have. We really shouldn't need the impulse drive anyway." She paused and then spoke in a serious voice. "Have the boat go to battle stations at 2300 hours, but don't sound battle stations. Have everyone awaken and go to their stations quietly. I'll see you on the conn."

"Excuse me, Helen, aren't you going to fill me in on the details?"

"Of course. We've been ordered to take out at least two carriers at all cost. That includes ramming, if necessary. This boat is considered expendable to accomplish that mission. Make sure all torpedoes tubes are loaded and ready to fire. Have fire control run diagnostics on all systems again, while you're at it. Remember, we haven't even fired a practice torpedo. Any questions?" Before Bill had a chance to answer she dismissed him and closed her door.

Chapter 9

Washington D.C. House Chamber
"Ladies and Gentleman. I have assembled this emergency session to call for a vote on a matter of grave importance, one that no one really wants, but has been thrust upon us. As you arrived here this evening, you saw an example of the Islamic Republic's ruthlessness. The United States of America, has been attacked twice by their regime. Yesterday, in international waters of the Mediterranean, the destroyer, USS John Rogers, was attacked and sunk with the loss of approximately half her crew of 523 men and women. The second was a two-pronged cowardly attack against the Pentagon with the death toll as high as 800 there, and to downtown Washington, with an unaccountably heavy loss of civilians. These two attacks were carried out by madmen!

We cannot allow this ruthlessness to continue to spread and gain strength! We must stop this plague before it's too late! They have already sealed off the Mediterranean, isolating Greece and Italy. Israel has been annihilated. I beseech you, members of Congress, do not repeat past errors and allow this oppressive force to continue terrorizing the world. Let us act now to halt this advance and drive the enemy into oblivion! Let us begin the march to the new, peaceful world that has so far eluded us!

I therefore ask you for a formal Declaration of War against the people who would end freedom of religion, freedom of speech and racial and sexual equality that we have worked so long and hard to obtain. I ask you for a formal Declaration of War against the Islamic Republic!"

As the President concluded his address and made his way from the chamber, the room echoed with cheers and applause. Once the President cleared the chamber, the Speaker of the House banged his gavel to bring the assembly to order. "Ladies and Gentleman of Congress, in view of the seriousness of this matter, debate over this bill is waved and an immediate vote will be taken. A two-thirds vote majority in both houses will be required to pass. This joint session of

Congress stands adjourned. Senators and Representatives will report to their chamber for a vote to commence in 30 minutes."

As the Congress voted, the President boarded a helicopter for Andrews Air Force Base. "Mr. President, what if Congress doesn't pass the bill?"

"Jenny, I don't think you have to worry about that. The Congressional leadership has assured me it will pass. If however, Farnsworth comes up with enough support to prevent adoption, tough! The operation will go ahead as scheduled. We'll give them something to think about, now, and bloody their damn nose!"

His Secretary, sitting next to the President said, "Mr. President, Sam is on the line."

He took the phone from her, "Yes Sam, what's up?"

"Mr. President, we just received news about the Republic fleet that was in the Pacific."

"Where is it?"

"Attacking Japan!"

"Damn! Contact Andrews, inform them to deploy the Pacific fleet. Also have them inform the Admirals of the status. Our ETA is twenty minutes, I want a full briefing as soon as we arrive."

USS Hunley

As the Hunley closed in on the Republic's fleet, the control room was bathed in an eerie red glow to allow the crew's eyes night vision. Helen sat on the raised platform of the control room and Bill stood at the fire control computer, waiting for Helen's firing orders. The intercom speaker broke the silence, "Conn, Sonar. We have multiple contacts at extreme range, bearing 350 degrees relative."

"Very well, Sonar." Helen replied, and turned to the Diving Officer, "Dive, come left to new heading of 073 degrees, reduce speed to ahead two-thirds."

"Coming left to a heading of 073 degrees, ringing up ahead two-thirds. Aye."

Helen turned to the person in the head set. "Phone talker, tell the Torpedo room to open all outer doors."

"Yes, ma'am."

After the message was relayed, Bill spoke up, "Lights indicate intermediate...tubes open."

"Dive, take us up to sixty-two feet."

"Sixty-two feet, aye, Captain. Planesman, five degrees up bubble. Chief, flood negative five thousand pounds." The boat slowly rose in the water. As the depth gauge passed sixty-five feet the Dive continued, "Zero the planes." After a short pause to observe that the depth gauge was steady, "Captain, holding at sixty-two feet."

"Up scope." Helen ordered and as the periscope rose, Helen stood and grabbed the handles and pulled them down. She pressed her eyes against the eyepiece, rapidly swung around looking in a complete circle before fixing on the sonar contacts. "Bill, designate this target for the cannon and tubes one and four." After a few seconds pause, Helen exclaimed, "Holy shit!"

"What is it, Captain?"

"Another carrier! Bill, designate this target for tubes two, three, five and six." She moved a little more to the right, "Designate target for tubes seven and ten." More movement, "Designate tubes eight and nine." Helen then flipped the handles up. "Down scope. Take her down to 150 feet, ahead standard. We'll hold eleven and twelve in case we miss the first time." Helen looked around the control room. Nervous faces looked back at her, for reassurance. She drew a deep breath and filled the crew in on the orders she had been given. "We have orders to sink or disable at least two carriers. Unfortunately, though, we're also expendable. However, we are going to take out two carriers, plus some of their escorts and live to tell about it." As she spoke, the fire control computer was busy imputing the data from sonar and the target designations, continually updating the firing solutions for each target. "Bill, it looks like we're really going to find out how good this baby of yours is."

"Captain, it'll be a long time before another boat will have such a maiden voyage, so we better make a good showing of it," Bill replied.

Andrews Air Force Base

"Thank you, Mr. Speaker." The President hung up the phone and turned to General Wish, "General send this message to all the armed forces. 'Congress has approved the Declaration of War. Perform your duties knowing that your country fully supports you and your mission. May God find favor in our cause and truly bless and protect you men and women as you enter harm's way. President Steven P. Jackson.' Okay, now deploy the rest of our forces, launch the satellites, then let's get on with the damn war!"

"Yes, sir," turning to look at his aide, "Captain, did you get all of that?"

"Yes, sir."

"Then, what are you waiting for? I'm tired of being blind." The Captain ran from the room, to the make-shift communications center. "Mr. President," said Mike, "we have the Reagan, accompanied by two English carriers, and one French, steaming south from England. The Bush is coming in from the west. They'll be launching attack aircraft within a half-hour. The F-122's should already be airborne and the Med fleet should be at the straits in about one hour. The Hunley should also be engaging the enemy fleet at any moment."

"What do you think our chances are?" The President asked, grimly.

"Well Sir, it depends on if the Hunley can take out two carriers with most of their planes on board and the F-122s get their licks in. If so, we have an excellent chance of winning this battle. However, if we lose even one carrier, we'll be in deeper shit than we already are. We can't afford to swap them carrier for carrier."

USS Reagan

"Captain, Radar reports multiple contacts approaching from the south."

"Damn it, they found us! Contact the CAG. Have him launch our interceptors, then standby to launch the attack planes. Notify the rest of the fleet."

USS Hunley

"Captain, range to carrier 4000 yards."

"Very well, standby to fire all weapons at 3000 yards."

World War III
The Beginning

Bridge of the destroyer USS Sampson, off Groton, Connecticut

"Secure the maneuvering watch. Man battle stations. Set condition Zebra." Reaching over to change the switch setting on the intercom system he continued, "Sonar, go active. If that sub is still in the area we'll make contact soon." The old skipper hung up the microphone, his eyes never leaving the open water stretching out before the ship. As they passed from the river into open water of the Atlantic, all eyes were searching for signs of an enemy submarine.

"All ahead full, bring us to starboard ten degrees," the Captain ordered.

"Captain, all stations report manned and ready."

"Very well. Helmsman, come twenty-five degrees to port."

As the ship swung around and steadied on it's new course, the silence of the bridge was shattered by an excited voice coming over the intercom, "High speed contacts closing! Bearing fifteen degrees off the starboard bow."

"That son of bitch is sitting on the bottom! All ahead flank, now! Smitty, fire tubes two and four, fifteen degrees relative, manually detonate at 2000 and 2500 yards."

"Aye, aye, sir." Commander Smith ran to the fire control station, set the firing coordinates and pushed the fire switches. "Tube two away, tube four away." As the weapons officer completed firing, the ship was sprayed by water from an explosion astern. The hands cheered, thinking they were safe, as the stern of the ship was lifted out of the water by a second torpedo exploding. The ship then dropped back into the water with enough force to submerge the stern to the main deck.

"Bridge, more high speed contacts approaching, same bearing!" Came the report from the phone talker.

"Back emergency! Helmsman bring the bow fifteen degrees to starboard"

A frantic voice broke over the intercom, "Bridge, Engineering. We've lost propulsion, both shafts are jammed!"

Two consecutive explosions were heard off the bow. "Captain, torpedoes have been detonated."

"Smitty, launch subrocks toward that same location."

"Captain, at this close of range we could also take damage."

Joel M. Fulgham

"Damn it, Smitty! In ten seconds this ship will be done for anyway!" With those dreaded words, Commander Smith fed the information into the fire control computer. The captain reached for the microphone and flipped the. "Attention all hands. This is the Captain. Abandon ship, all hands abandon ship to port."

"Captain, launching subrocks."

"Smitty, wait." Before the Commander could respond, the ship shuttered violently and was lifted out of the water from explosions under her mid section. She paused for a moment, then came crashing back down with the sound of twisting metal signifying that her back had been broken. As the Captain and the bridge crew crawled to their feet, the Captain yelled, "Now Smitty. Launch everything we've got! Then get the hell out of here!"

"Yes Sir, launching." He got to his knees and pushed all the firing buttons. After a brief pause for the launch sequences to operate Smitty called, "Confirmation of four missiles launched." The commander struggled to his feet and looked at the Captain attempting to stand defiantly on the slanting deck while the rest of the crew ran to leave the dying ship. "Captain, we've done all we can. It's time to go."

The Captain slowly turned to look at the man telling him to leave his ship. The shock of what had happened to his ship made him incoherent, "Smitty, it's okay. You go ahead with the rest of the crew. I'll bring her back when I've sunk that sneaky little bastard."

"Jim, she's done! The Sampson's a dead, ship, sinking!"

"No, you're wrong, Smitty. She won't leave me. We've been together for too long a time, and she won't let me down now, not in our moment of glory."

"Jim, I hate to do this." Smitty's mighty right cross sent Jim tumbling backwards, hitting his head on the console. Lifting the limp body over his shoulder, Smitty managed to make his way outside and into the water just as the missiles exploded on the other side of the ship. After swimming a safe distance from the settling ship, Smitty turned in time to see it split in half and sink in the middle of the channel. Only the top of the mast remained above water to mark her grave. When the ripples in the water subsided, more men could be seen beyond the ship in the water. "Jim, you got her."

Andrews Air Force Base

"General, we have a flash message from Commander, Naval Base, Groton."

Mike turned and looked at the Lieutenant for a moment. "Well, Lieutenant, speak up. What's it say?"

"The destroyer, USS Sampson, has been sunk by an enemy submarine in the middle of the channel. Access to and from the base is blocked until the Sampson can be removed. They are currently dispatching long boats to pick up survivors."

Mike slowly turned to Steve. "Looks like we found one of the subs you've been hunting. What do you want to do now?"

After a few seconds of thought, Steve spoke up, "Lieutenant, send the following to all Atlantic Bases: Do not deploy ships until further notice. Maintain at hot standby. You are to deploy anti-submarine aircraft and concentrate search to the transport channels of Naval bases. Next send this on a secure channel to Commander, Naval Base Groton: Admiral Jordan, find and destroy that submarine. Use saturation with depth charges if necessary. Then clear your channel by blowing up the Sampson. Dispatch destroyer groups to as many ports as possible to assist in clearing them. Do not use groups smaller than four destroyers. Good luck. CNO, Admiral Steve Schmidt." Steve turned to Mike, "Damn, I can't believe they beat us to again."

Just then another radio operator jumped in, "Admiral, the Reagan's broken radio silence and reports contact with enemy fighters. All carriers are launching to engage."

"Steve, what were you saying about beating us to the punch? Let's pray that the Hunley can act real soon," Mike said, sounding desperate.

Chapter 10

USS Hunley

"Captain, range to target one is 3050 yards."

"Commence firing at 3000 yards, fire at five second intervals. Cannon fire control, standby to fire on my mark."

The control room took on a nervous silence as the crew waited for the order. "3020 yards to target."

"Very well. Bill, commence firing."

"Fire one." Then a five second pause. "Fire four."

Then Helen broke in, "Fire the cannon." The lights dimmed briefly and returned to normal. "No pop, good job, Bill." Just as Helen finished this comment a rumble echoed through the boat. "Sounds like we hit something out there."

Bill was oblivious to her comments as well as the commotion around him as he continued to count for the firing of the torpedoes. He looked at the fire control computer. "Eight seconds on number one's run." He started his new count down, "Five, four, three, two, one." The sounds of a distant explosion filled the boat. Before it was completely gone another sound wave echoed through the boat.

"Bill, what's the run time to the next target?"

Bill glanced up at the fire control computer, "Twelve seconds, Captain."

The sonar operator broke in, "Captain sounds like missiles are being launched."

"All ahead flank, emergency deep. Make your depth 1000 feet."

"Captain, Sonar, picking up more torpedo hits. Should be the second carrier. Hold it! Picking up two splashes dead astern. High-speed screws starting up. They have gone active. They appear to be going away."

"Very well. Dive, slow to ahead two-thirds. Bring us up to periscope depth."

"Captain, all of our torpedoes for target two have detonated." Bill interrupted.

"Captain, sonar reports new sounds. Appears to be a destroyer closing fast. They are active on sonar."

"Mark the bearing."

"260 degrees relative."

"Dive hard to port 80 degrees! Cannon control, lock in on that target!" The boat banked slightly as she came around to her new heading and continued her accent to periscope depth. Sound of more distant explosions filled the boat as her torpedoes continued to find their targets.

"Captain, we are at periscope depth, steady on heading, 353 degrees."

"Up scope." As the scope came up Helen grabbed the handles and made a quick 360 degree scan of the area before stopping to look straight ahead.

"Captain, our scope has been detected by enemy radar."

"Stay with me, bearing mark."

The 1st Class Petty Officer standing opposite Helen glanced at the position indicator and replied "negative two degrees."

Helen then made another adjustment, "Range mark."

Again checking out the settings, "two five double oh."

"Cannon control fire! Down scope! Crash dive, all ahead flank! Sound collision!" The lights repeated their dimming act as the cannon fired. Helen reached over and picked up the microphone. "This is the Captain. While we were at periscope depth an enemy destroyer got a good radar fix on us. It's going to get a little rough in the next few minutes, so everybody hold tight." As she finished, she hung the microphone up and grabbed onto one of the poles that surrounded the conn.

"Captain! High speed screws coming in dead ahead! Wait, more splashes, more high speed screws."

"Launch counter measures!" She looked at Bill," I hope you built this boat real sturdy." She said as she gave him a wink. Suddenly the boat was rocked violently by a series of nearby explosions. In the sonar shack, the sonar operators grabbed at their headphones, as the lights went out momentarily. When the emergency lights came on, "Phone-talker, get me a damage report from Maneuvering."

Joel M. Fulgham

"Yes, ma'am." The phone-talker spoke into his headset. After a few moments the reply came back, "Maneuvering reports flooding from a busted seawater line. Flooding has been stopped. But it shorted out the main, electrical switchboards. There's a loss of AC power and the reactor plant has been shut down. We'll have emergency propulsion restored in a few minutes."

"Bill, go to engineering and help get us back into the battle."

"Yes, Ma'am." Bill looked over his shoulder at the woman standing behind him, "Lieutenant, take over for me."

"Chief, can we maintain depth control?"

"I'll let you know in a few minutes."

"Phone talker get damage reports from the rest of the boat." Helen finally had the chance to observe the condition of the control room. In the dimly-lit space, debris was scattered across the floor, from navigation charts to broken coffee cups. Several of the crew were rubbing various parts of their bruised bodies. For the most part, though, everything seemed intact. Out of the corner of her eye, she noticed water running down the periscope. "Well, there goes any more periscope attacks," she thought to herself.

At that moment, the phone talker interrupted her thoughts. "With the exception of sonar, all stations report no major damage to any operational equipment."

Helen spoke, "What does sonar report?"

"They do not reply."

"Messenger, go to the sonar shack and find out what's going on in there."

"Yes, ma'am." In a few seconds, the messenger returned, "Captain, they're all unconscious."

"Phone talker, contact damage control and have them provide sonar operators. And have the corpsman lay to the sonar shack."

"Captain, depth is 843 feet and maintaining."

"Captain, Mr. Floyd is in engineering and would like to talk to you on the phone."

"Thank you." Helen reached for the handset. "Yes, Bill."

"Captain, this mess is going to take awhile to square away. Several breakers need to be replaced, since they burnt up from the short, so we'll have to use the diesel for enough power to start backup. Also, the flooding came from the diesel seawater system, so it has to be repaired before we can start the reactor again. Therefore, we need to get our butts out of here so we can snorkel the diesel."

"Alright, we'll get us to safer waters."

Helen hung up the handset and the word came, "Captain, sonar reports manned and ready. They report distant explosions."

"Very well. Phone talker. Relay this message to the crew. We have accomplished our mission and the enemy fleet should now be under attack by F-122s. If they're as successful as we've been, the Republic's fleet will be down to a manageable size. Now, we're pulling back to make repairs before we can re-engage the enemy. My gratitude goes to each of you for the way you've performed your duties."

USS Reagan

"Captain, our planes have engaged enemy fighters at 120 nautical miles out. Radio also reports the F-122s have engaged the enemy fleet."

"Well, it looks like we might have a chance after all."

"Captain, radar indicates more planes are coming from Spain. Our planes from France and England are vectoring to intercept. However, I don't think they can intercept before they reach us."

"CAG, what do we have available to meet this threat?"

"Just one squadron and our C.A.P."

"Dispatch them to engage."

"That'll leave us with no protection."

The Captain glared with irritation at the CAG and said, "Look, Commander. If those planes get within range, we won't need any protection!"

"Yes Sir." Turning to his radio operator, he issued the order.

Andrews Air force Base

"General, we're receiving pictures from the satellite."

"It's about time. Let me see them immediately."

The radio operator broke in. "General, the Med fleet reports they've run into heavy opposition at Gibraltar. The Republic stationed a battleship and escorts in the way."

"Contact France and see if they can bomb that battleship." Then turning to look at Steve, "Shit! That's another wrinkle we didn't expect."

"The fleet isn't lost yet," Steve injected. "Radio, Contact the Hunley. Have them engage that battleship."

"Yes, sir."

An airman entered the room carrying photographs. "General, here are the pictures you wanted."

"It's about time. Steve, come over here." The two men walked to a large table set against the wall and studied the pictures for a few minutes. "Shit! Eight carriers," the General murmured. He addressed the messenger, "How old are these pictures?"

"A little over thirty minutes, sir."

"At least we know what they started with. Lieutenant, contact intelligence and tell them we need updated pictures, ASAP. Steve, what do you think?"

"If we're able to concentrate our fighter attacks on the carriers, we can come out in good shape. However, since we have to defend against their land-based planes too, it's not going to be easy. If our planes can break through and attack their fleet it'll be a miracle. I think we have to depend on the Hunley and F-122s to cut their fleet down a bit."

"Mike, look at this shot, here's the problem at Gibraltar, a battleship flanked by four frigates, all in position for a broadside shot on anything trying to come through."

"Admiral, we have radio contact with Admiral Mora on the Reagan. He wishes to speak to you."

"Where can I take it?"

"Over here, sir," the Lieutenant pointed to one of the radio stations that had been set up.

"Mike, wanna hear this?"

"You betcha!" He asked the Sergeant in charge, "Can you put it on the speaker?"

The Sergeant tapped the operator on his shoulder. "Put it on." The operator flipped a switch and the speaker crackled slightly as it came to life. "USS Reagan, this is Admiral Schmidt, go ahead."

World War III
The Beginning

A few moments of tense silence followed before Admiral Mora was heard. "Steve, I'm sorry, but I've had to order a retreat. Our fighters are outnumbered by at least five-to-one and can't keep the enemy away from the fleet. The Phalanx systems of our screens are running dry from beating off enemy fighters and missiles. Casualties, so far, are three destroyers damaged, one destroyer and one frigate disabled and one destroyer sunk. One of the carriers was hit and its flight deck is inoperable. The Sir Lancelot is burning, but her Captain thinks they can control it and get back to England. Best estimate so far, is that we've lost about one-fourth of our aircraft. Sorry to let you down, sir. The good news is that our fighters that got close enough to observe the enemy, reported two carriers and several other ships burning."

"Andy, you did the best you could. Continue pulling back to safe water." Steve took a deep breath and let it out with a heavy sigh. "Sorry, Mike, looks like our carriers struck out and took a beating at the same time. But at least the Hunley did her part. We hope that while our carriers had their fighters engaged, the F-122s were successful."

"Don't take it so hard, Steve. It looks like the enemy knew we were coming."

Finally, an excited voice vibrated through the hanger. "Mike, we just heard from the base commander in Paris. One of the F-122 squadrons has reported in. As they were approaching the enemy, there were explosions on the far side of the fleet. After they delivered their payload, they did a quick flyby of the area. A destroyer was launching antisubmarine missiles, then exploded. They observed a large amount of debris and people in the water. They also report losing only one plane while sinking one carrier, damaging another and a heavy cruiser."

"Thanks for that good news, John, but we already heard it from the Reagan. Steve, I hope the Hunley came through, but it doesn't sound like we should count on her to engage that battleship. Has anyone heard if we've gotten any assistance to the Med Fleet yet?"

"No, sir. Paris says they can't get any planes down there for at least two hours."

Joel M. Fulgham

Another radio operator interrupted, "Admiral, Commander Naval Base Groton reports the enemy sub was sunk by the Sampson before she went down. The rescue boats have picked up several of its survivors along with survivors of the Sampson. He also reports a Seal team is preparing to look for survivors trapped in air pockets on the Sampson. If no more survivors are found, they'll plant explosives on the wreck and clear the channel."

"Thank you Corporal." Steve looked at Mike, "More good news in this night of disaster, one down, two to go."

Chapter 11

USS Hunley

Helen had planned to turn over the conn when she reached safe water. However, their new orders forced her to change those plans. She remained on the conn using her willpower to keep the boat moving toward their new target as the crew busily repaired the battle damage. Helen and the crew knew they would be walking a fine line for the next hour or so. Picking up the mike, she punched the button for engineering, "Maneuvering, conn. How's our battery power holding up?"

"We're down to fifty percent reserve. At the current use, we'll be dead in the water in sixty-seven minutes."

"Very well," was Helen's response. Then, turning to the Navigator, "Nav, how long to target?"

"In firing range in twenty minutes."

Helen hastily calculated what battery power would be left if she had to use the cannon in the upcoming battle. She figured that after firing the cannon, the boat would have about ten minutes left on the battery and their hope for survival would be to disable all five enemy ships with torpedoes. If they have to use the cannon, they'd stop dead in the water and be blasted to pieces. "Nav, take the conn, steady as she goes. I'll be in Engineering."

"Yes, ma'am." The young Lieutenant stepped onto the platform.

Helen, hit the deck at a run on her way aft. As she moved through the tunnel, she saw a group working at the far end and yelled, "Make a hole!" Once through the group, she hurried to Maneuvering. Upon reaching the ten-by-twenty-foot, air-conditioned box known as maneuvering, Helen barged in. Upon entering, she felt a rush of cold air hit her in the face, in sharp contrast to the one hundred plus temperatures of the other engineering spaces. "Why the hell is it so cold in here? Ensign, turn that blower off, damn it!"

"Yes, Captain, but I'm a Lieutenant JG."

"Correction - you were a JG. Get the Engineer in here, NOW!"

The man picked up the mike and requested the Engineering Officer to come to Maneuvering on the double.

When the Engineer showed up, he stuck his head in, "Request permission to enter. Oh, hi, Captain. Why's it so cold in here?"

"Commander, I want this man relieved of his current duties and assigned to the hottest and dirtiest job possible."

The Engineer glowered at the man who was in tears and coldly said, "You are relieved. Step outside and wait at attention." With that, the cowed young officer moved outside. "Captain, what else can I do for you?"

"How long until we can start the reactor plant up?"

"We're working on the last breakers now. But, we then have to test them, so I estimate another two hours."

"What if we skip testing and override all the protective features? How long to get to full power then?"

"Captain, if we get everything operational, go directly to pulling rods, and everything works perfectly, about an hour. But, Captain, there are some other problems. The crew is getting sluggish from the heat. I'm afraid if we keep pushing them like we have, they'll start collapsing from heat stroke."

"That's easy, punch up the conn and hand me the mike. "Conn, this is the Captain. Have all personnel not involved in repairs carry pitchers of ice water and buckets of cool water to the engineering spaces on the double." Releasing the button, Helen instructed the Engineer to switch to the announcing. "Attention, this is the Captain. I understand your discomfort from the heat, but you know how important it is that these repairs be completed as soon as possible. To help cool you off as much as possible, ice water is on its way to you. Buckets of cool water are also on their way aft to pour over you and help lower your body temperature. This is no time for modesty, so if you feel it will help you to keep cool, you have permission to remove whatever clothing you feel would help." Turning to the Engineer, "That's is all we can do to help, without stopping work. Now, for what I came back here for, I need more power and time. We need to shut down everything possible. And, I do mean everything, from the scrubbers to the air conditioning plants. As it is now, if we fire the cannon, we will have about ten minutes of power left."

"Captain, you realize that'll mean losing the navigation equipment in a matter of minutes."

"Yes, but we have to help get our Med Fleet out. Once that's accomplished, they can escort us until we can get our equipment operational again."

"Okay, Captain, I'll do what I can."

The ship's announcing system came to life, "Captain to the conn. Firing range in ten minutes." Helen looked at the Engineer, "Get me the time I need. Okay?" Exiting the compartment, she bumped into Bill. "Are you done here?"

"I think they can finish without me. Shall we go sink some ships?"

"I'm glad you can join me for this. I need you at weapons control. We can't raise the scope so we'll have to do it by sonar alone. Think you can handle it?"

"Yeah, I think so. If not, the torpedoes can go active and acquire the targets themselves."

"No. We have to make sure we hit all five ships. If the torpedoes acquire on their own, they may all hit the same ship."

"I know that, but chances are they'll hit at least four of them. If we miss one, the cannon will take care of it. You're worried about battery power and don't want to use the cannon, right?"

"Right. I don't. If we use the cannon, we'll only have about ten minutes of power left."

"I have an idea. Once we close within range, we kill propulsion and hover."

"That would buy us some time wouldn't it. Alright! What are we waiting for, Let's do it!"

On their way forward, they passed crewmembers hard at work on their equipment and in various stages of undress, anywhere from jumper tops rolled down and tied around their waist, to their skivvies. Two men stood back and watched a female who had slipped her jumpsuit down to her waist and was now wearing merely a sweaty-clingy t-shirt. Helen interrupted them by clearing her voice. The two men quickly turned as she continued, "Excuse me gentlemen, don't you two have work to do?"

"Yes Ma'am." one stammered as they turned back to their assigned jobs. Just then the one guy that's in every crowd came walking around the corner wearing absolutely nothing. "Oh shit," was all he could get out as he attempted to cover his private parts.

"Well, Petty Officer Bivins, I hope you're nice and cool now. Be careful not to get too close to any steam pipes." Helen said as her eyes drifted up and down.

Bill was about to say something about at least wearing skivvies, but Helen interrupted, "Bill, I gave permission for them to do whatever's necessary to stay cool and that's what he's doing. As long as none of crew complains, I don't have a problem with it. Carry on, Bivins." They headed to the control room.

As they entered the control room there was a scrapping sound on the outside of the hull. Bill shouted, "All stop!" Turning to Helen, "Sounds like mine cables."

"Dive, center your rudder, take us back, dead slow."

Again the scrapping sound came from the bow of the boat, then faded away. "All stop. What side did that sound like to you, Bill?"

"Port, I think."

"I agree. Dive, bring us five degrees to starboard, ten degree rise on the planes, ahead slow. Make your depth six-five feet. Do not use the pumps to adjust trim on the boat."

"Aye, aye, Captain." As the boat slowly climbed toward the surface and pushed forward, all ears strained to hear the scrapping sound. It never recurred.

Finally Helen picked up the microphone and ordered sonar to feed their data to the fire control.

"Captain, do you want us to set the fish for seeking or try to use the data we have?" Bill knew she didn't want to use seek so he added another suggestion. "We could use the data we already have and designate targets. Then just before we shoot, use a single ping from the active sonar for a positive fix."

"Okay, target two fish each at what we believe are the cruisers and four at the battleship."

"Yes, ma'am." Bill turned to the weapons operator and instructed her to key in targeting for each of the twelve tubes. Bill was confident this would work, but was worried that they might not be able to surface when it was all over. The Hunley had already fired ten torpedoes. Now, if they fire the next twelve, will that leave them enough air in the air banks to blow the water out of the ballast tanks. It is very likely they will not have enough propulsion power to push them to the surface. "Captain, targeting computer has the firing instructions."

"Very well. Dive, all stop." Keying the mike, Helen issued the order. "Sonar, this is the Captain. Initiate active sonar for one, I repeat, one pulse and feed the data directly to the fire control computer."

Helen and Bill looked directly into each other's eyes as they waited to hear the ping. Then through the breathless silence it came. "PING." Within seconds the targeting computer operator spoke up, "Positive lock on targets. Nearest target 1000 yards. By the size of it, it's the battleship!"

Helen rapidly fired out, "Bill, fire all tubes, three second intervals." Then turning to the young seaman wearing the sound powered phones, "Phone talker, inform the torpedo room to load our last two fish in tubes one and two as soon as possible."

"Yes, ma'am."

"Cannon fire control, are you ready if required?"

"Manned and ready, Captain. Just give the word."

"Maintain your firing rate, Petty Officer Desmond," Bill ordered as he turned to talk to Helen. "Captain, we should hit targets one and three in rapid succession. Followed by two, four and five."

"Ten away...eleven away...twelve away. All fish are away, running normally and on target," announced Petty Officer Desmond.

"Five seconds, left on run to first target," Bill continued as he started his count down to the first hits. "Three, two, one!" As he finished counting the submarine reverberated with the sound of a series of six explosions.

"Captain, sonar reports the sound of screws starting up," the phone talker chimed in as the sounds of two more explosions were heard.

"Captain, fish one through eight have detonated. Six seconds left till number nine. Four, three, two, one!" As Bill finished yet another distant explosion echoed through the boat. Three seconds later the second torpedo found its home in the ship.

"XO, how much longer for the last target?"

"Coming up on five, four, three, two, one!" No explosion this time.

The phone talker was the first one to speak up, "Captain, sonar reports a destroyer closing fast, bearing 340 degrees relative. Second contact, heavy screws closing at a slower speed, it could be the battleship."

Before Helen could respond the Diving Officer cut in, "Captain, we can no longer maintain depth control. We are going down, eighty feet and increasing."

"Dive, ring up the minimum speed required to maintain depth control."

"Aye, aye. Ringing up ahead slow."

Helen then spun around to look at the cannon operator, "Cannon control, can you lock in on the closest target?"

"Give me one second. Locked in on target, Captain."

"Fire!"

"Pulse away!" Within seconds the force of an explosion once again rocked the boat.

"Dive, take us down to the bottom," Helen ordered. As the boat descended, the sound of the battleship passing overhead vibrated through the boat.

"Captain, Sonar reports the battleship is dropping depth charges. They also report that the destroyer is dead in the water."

"Captain, ringing up all stop. We are about five feet off the bottom, settling slowly."

The phone talker spoke. "Captain, the Engineer wants you on the phone."

Before Helen could pick up the phone, the intercom came to life, "Conn, Torpedo room. Tubes one and two loaded and ready to fire."

World War III
The Beginning

Helen looked to Bill, "target tubes one and two for that battleship." She then picked up the microphone, "Standby for depth charges." She hung up the mike and picked up the phone, "Yes."

"Captain, if we don't increase power usage, we have battery power for only thirty minutes. If we have to use propulsion again at one third, a mere fifteen minutes. And remember, that time is decreasing every second."

"Thanks." The Captain looked at her watch as the boat gave a slight shudder as she settled on the bottom and rolled five degrees to port.

"Captain, we have a firing solution."

"Very well. Fire tubes one and two!"

Bill nodded at Petty Officer Desmond, and she pushed the firing buttons. "Captain, fish are away and running normally."

"Bill, come here."

As Bill walked around to the steps, the boat was violently rocked by the depth charges detonating above them. The Navigator spoke up. "Captain, our navigation equipment just died."

Petty Officer Desmond started the count down for the torpedo run, "three, two, one." As if on cue, the sound of the torpedoes hitting their target echoed throughout the boat.

When Bill stepped beside Helen, she whispered, "We can't run and, we may not be able to blow ourselves to the surface. There's a battleship above us, dropping depth charges. And to make matters worse, only thirty minutes of battery life left. Any suggestions?"

Before Bill could answer, the speaker came to life, "Conn, Sonar. Multiple contacts dead ahead, closing at high speed. It could be the fleet coming through, because the battleship is moving off."

Helen picked up the mike, "Very well, Sonar." Helen took a deep breath, and whispered, "thank you," as she looked up. Then turning to the Diving Officer, "Dive, perform an emergency blow on all main ballast tanks!"

"Emergency blow, aye. Chief of the Watch, hit the chicken switch." The Chief jumped up and moved the levers that released high-pressure air into the main ballast tanks. As the air rushed in the boat gave a momentary shuddered, then nothing. She remained stuck to the bottom of the sea.

"Chief hit it again," Helen ordered. The Chief again moved the lever and looked over at the pressure gauge on the tanks. "Captain, there is no pressure decrease on the air banks. The valves must be frozen."

Helen turned to Bill, "Okay, mister, she's your baby, what do you suggest?"

"Well Captain, I don't think that the problem is we're too heavy. More likely we're stuck in the mud. I suggest going to full raise on the planes then ahead standard on the impulse drive that's working. Maybe the force of the water leaving will break the mud's suction. Then we'll shoot to the top."

"If it doesn't work we'll be down here without power. What then?" Helen queried.

"The way I see it, if we don't break free, we'll be down here without power anyway."

"Good point," Helen replied as she reached for the microphone. "Maneuvering, this is the Captain. Shift propulsion to the impulse drive."

After waiting a few tense minutes that seemed to stretch out for an eternity, a reply came back, "Control Room, Maneuvering, ready to answer bells using the impulse drive."

"Okay, let's do it. Dive full rise on the planes, ahead standard." As the pump came up to speed, the boat rocked forward then back. Ever so slowly she inched forward, then stopped. Repeating the process several times, the Hunley finally broke free from the grasp of the mud and moved ahead and up. The phone talker spoke up, "Captain, maneuvering reports the batteries are dead!"

"Dive, report!"

"Still gaining vertical speed, passing 300 feet. Reducing to fifteen degree rise."

"Captain, Sonar reports we're headed directly for the fleet!"

"Helmsman hard to port! Bring us around 180 degrees by magnetic compass. Phone talker have all station prepare to snorkel," Helen was struggling to maintain her composure. "Damn, we can't use the radio! Messenger go to radio and have someone get in here with a signal light."

World War III
The Beginning

"Captain, we just lost external hydraulics, we have no plane or rudder control! Passing 200 feet...100 feet," the Diving Officer report.

"Bill, manually raise the snorkel mast!" As members of the crew struggled with the pumps to raise the snorkel mast, the Hunley burst from below the waves like a breaching whale, with half her length shooting out of the water, then crashing down with a tremendous splash. The resulting white water was clearly visible in the moonlight. "Cracking the Hatch!" Helen shouted as she jumped from the conn to the ladder leading up and spun the handle wheel. Her ears clogged up as air rushed out as she loosened the hatch lowering the air pressure inside the boat.

"All stations report ready to snorkel."

A radioman hustled into the control room carrying a signal light. "Commence snorkeling, lookouts and radioman lay topside." As Helen issued the orders, Bill grabbed the binoculars hanging next to the ladder and rushed up behind her. Two seamen and the radioman followed them closely. Once topside, they could identify the outline of the approaching ships. Bill whispered, "I hope they can see us." Helen opened the water-tight box of the communication equipment, "Maneuvering, forget a warmup on the diesel, just get it on line." Helen hung up. "They're bringing the diesel on line now. Bill, put on the headset so that we can get this thing moving in a hurry."

Maneuvering immediately came on the phone to inform them the diesel was supplying power. "Captain, the diesel is on line."

"Alright then, ahead two thirds. Also have radio come back on line and inform the fleet we are here and need assistance. Have maneuvering restart the external hydraulic pumps."

"Yes, ma'am," As Bill relayed the message to radio, a bright flash appeared on one of the approaching ships followed by the boom of a four inch gun being fired and the splash of a shell landing in the water about twenty yards to starboard. "Shit! Get that light working and signal them who we are!" The radioman started flashing Morse code to the approaching ships.

Bill received a disheartening reply over the phones, "Bridge, Radio. We have power, will be able to send in a couple of minutes."

Bill relayed the message to Helen, "Captain, Radio says it'll take a few minutes to get operational."

"Damn, we don't have a few minutes!" Helen replied with irritation.

"Message sent, Captain."

As they waited for a reply another flash appeared from the approaching ship, followed by another splash closer to starboard. Then a light flashed from the approaching ship. "Whew, they've finally acknowledged us."

"Captain, Radio reports they are sending and receiving. Maneuvering reports we have hydraulics and limited propulsion."

"Thank goodness. Bill you have the Conn. I'm going below to radio. Reduce speed to one-third so we can charge the battery faster. Then she looked Bill straight in the eyes, "We make a pretty good team, don't we." She gave him a wink and a smile.

"Yes, ma'am," he smiled back. After she left, Bill reduced the boat's speed to a one-third bell, which allowed the fleet to close on them faster. As the night progressed, the fleet overtook the Hunley and four destroyers huddled around her. The lead ship threw a towline so the Hunley could kill its propulsion and allow her to divert more power to charging the battery. The destroyer was able to pull her faster so they could clear the area in better time. Once clear of the straits, the group headed southwest.

As dawn began to break, the Hunley had regained sufficient power to re-start the reactor and restore full power. By the following night, all systems were fully operational and they were ready to leave the protection of the destroyers. After Helen expressed her thanks to the other ships' skippers, she issued orders, "Officer of the Deck, take her down to five hundred feet." The boat submerged and as they passed one hundred feet, Helen gave the command, "Dive, ahead full. Nav, give me a heading for the Azores."

"Aye, Captain." The Navigator did some rapid calculations and replied, "Three-two-five, Captain."

"Officer of the Deck, bring her starboard to a new heading of three-two-five. Once we're at 500 feet, go to ahead, flank. I'll be in radio, then my cabin if you need me." At the radio shack's door, she entered her access code into the security lock and stepped inside.

"Chief, send this message to the Commodore aboard the Cable. 'Temporary repairs completed. Making best speed to rendezvous at point Bravo. Require full load of fish. I also wish to propose a commendation for each member of the crew. Commanding Officer, USS Hunley. Send that as soon as possible, Chief."

"Yes, ma'am. Consider it already done."

"Thank, you. Oh, and no one else is to know about this, Okay?" The Chief Petty Officer nodded in reply and gave her a wide grin and wink.

In her cabin, door closed, Helen sat in her chair and meditated on the occurrences of the past few days-all the decisions she and Bill made that allowed the Hunley to survive. "What if Bill had not been there to offer his ideas? What would her decisions have been? What would have been the fate of the Hunley?" Slowly, without noticing, she compared Bill to her old friend and lover, Matt. Though not physically Matt's equal, Bill had other qualities she found intriguing. He was able to anticipate her questions and have an answer ready before she asked. She wondered if he could read her thoughts and anticipate her desires in other areas. After an hour or so, she slowly undressed for bed, her thoughts still on Bill. After crawling into her bunk, she curled up with a pillow and was soon fast asleep.

0400 Hunley

"Captain, this is the Conn," came over the speaker above Helen's bunk. She struggled to open her eyes while fumbling to find the switch that would allow her to reply. "Go ahead."

"You have an incoming message from the Commodore."

"Have the messenger hang it on my door."

"Yes ma'am, will do."

Helen lied there for another moment, trying to focus her mind. Slowly, she threw the covers back and sat up, her feet on the floor. After a long stretch, she half-stumbled to the head door, and turned the knob. What greeted her brought her instantly fully awake. Bill was naked, drying himself after a shower, staring back at his naked captain. Helen regained her composure, quickly closed the door as Bill wrapped the towel around himself. He gathered up his shower bag and knocked on the door, "Captain, its open," and quickly left through the door to his cabin.

Bill sat on the edge of his bunk for a few moments as his pulse returned to normal, all the while thinking about what had happened and what he'd say when they next met. As he slowly dressed, he kept thinking about her until there was a knock on the head door. He reached over and opened it. "Come in, Captain."

Helen entered, her coveralls zipped to just above her breasts, which was lower than he'd ever seen it, or, he thought, was he just noticing more now? "Bill, I received a message from the Commodore. We're to rendezvous with the Cable for a one-week refit, and we'll be taking on thirty more people. So, while we're making repairs, we need to come up with a way of making sleeping arrangements for everyone. It may require hot bunking many of the crew. And there will be two officers included, so make room for them in Officer Country."

"Right. I'll take care of it."

Helen turned, started back to her cabin, then looked over her shoulder and said, "Nice," as she walked through the door and shut it behind her.

Chapter 12

USS Cable

The Commodore was at his desk, studying charts, when he was disturbed by a knock on the door. "Enter."

"Excuse me, sir. The Hunley has tied up alongside."

"Thank you, Small. Please tell her Captain and Executive Officer to report to me immediately."

"Aye, aye, sir," snapped the young man as he softly closed the door on his way out. The Commodore returned to his charts as he sipped a cup of coffee.

Topside on the Hunley

Petty Officer Small climbed down the long ladder from the Cable's main deck to the Hunley. He stopped at the rope across the ladder that read, 'Security Area.' An armed Petty Officer stood at the sign in his summer whites, to verify that everyone boarding the submarine had the appropriate security clearances and authorization. Small delivered the Commodore's request and retreated back up the ladder. The Petty Officer relayed the message below.

Helen and Bill were in the wardroom, looking over the list of needed repairs when the messenger entered, "Excuse me Captain. The Commodore would like to see the two of you in his stateroom immediately."

Helen looked up at the seaman, "Very well. Tell the Officer of Day where we'll be."

"Yes, ma'am."

"I wonder what's so important?" Bill asked.

"Your guess is as good as mine. But let's not keep the man waiting," Helen replied, as they both stood and headed to the tender.

Commodore's Stateroom

Helen knocked on the door, slowly opened it and stuck her head in. There was no one in the room. She opened the door all the way and walked in, Bill close behind. Once both were in, a curtain at the side was flung open with people behind it yelling, "SURPRISE!"

89

Joel M. Fulgham

Helen and Bill both jumped. When she regained her poise, Helen asked what the occasion was?

The Commodore stepped forward, his hand outstretched, "To congratulate you and your crew on a smashing victory over the Republic. Your success in combat not only enabled the Med fleet to escape, but sufficiently crippled the Republic's fleet to allow our combined U.S., English and French fleet to safely withdraw. You caused so much havoc, they were forced to use a significant portion of their ships to try and find you. Oh, and I almost forgot, happy birthday, Commander."

Helen face began to redden as she smiled at the Commodore and looked around at the other faces smiling back. "Thank you, sir. I really don't know what to say. We were given a job to do and we did it. That's all."

"Don't be so modest, Helen. You and your crew did more than anyone could ask," The Commodore boomed back. "The President also sends his thanks. Because of you, we have more time to firm up our forces while the Republic regroups."

"Unfortunately, though, we also have some bad news," he continued. "The Republic has been bombing Japan's factories and we haven't yet moved to engage them. That means we'll be short of some parts for a while. The President has ordered American industries to gear up to produce these parts. We hope full production can start before our current supply is exhausted. Also, the Republic has complete control of Portugal, Israel and Spain. Without our fleet in the Med, invasion of the remaining Mediterranean countries is certain."

"Is there a plan to strengthen the resistance?" Helen interrupted.

The Commodore looked sadly at her before answering, "I'm almost sorry to answer, yes. But you'll hear more about it at tomorrows meeting."

"What meeting?" Helen replied.

"The one on Santa Cruz that you, Bill and myself will attend. We'll leave by launch at 1800 hours tonight for the island. Tomorrow, at 0800 hours, we'll meet with Admiral Schmidt and the commanders of the Carrier groups to discuss how best to proceed. In the meantime,

World War III
The Beginning

I recommend your crew receive R and R on the Island of Corvo. Since the Portuguese Government is no longer, we figured we would set up a temporary base there, complete with bar."

"But Sir, we have only one week before we sail," Helen reminded him.

"I'm well aware of that, but after what you and your crew have been through, you deserve a couple of days rest. The tender crew will make your required repairs. Therefore, I suggest each crewmember be given two days on the island. Now, have some birthday cake, then go take care of your business on the Hunley and be back here at 1745 hours, ready for a couple of relaxing days on Santa Cruz."

Helen looked at the Commodore curiously and replied, "Yes, sir. Whatever you say, sir." She picked up a plate of cake, a glass of punch and entered into conversation with the other officers in the stateroom. Shortly thereafter, she and Bill said their goodbyes and left.

During their walk back to the Hunley, Helen decided the crew would take their liberty in port and starboard duty sections. Port section would have the first duty and starboard would have two days off on the island of Corvo. Then they would switch. That way they would still have three days with a full crew to prepare for sea again. She also stated that the Engineering Officer, Lt. Commander Mackie, would fill in for them while they were Santa Cruz.

When they reached the Hunley, Helen asked Mackie to come to her in her cabin, then headed below. When she reached her cabin, Mackie was already there. "The XO and I have to attend a meeting in Santa Cruz tomorrow. We'll be leaving tonight at 1800 hours and return in two days. You will be in command during that time. The tender people will be doing most of the repairs, so all the crew will have to do is support them. Each member of the port and starboard duty sections will get two days on another island. You'll go when we get back. Any questions?"

"No, ma'am. I can handle it. You just get as much rest as you can. I have a feeling you made need it."

"Thanks, Eng. I'll try."

Meanwhile, Bill headed to the Chief Petty Officer berthing, called the "Goat Locker," to inform the Chief of the Boat, known as the "COB", of the arrangements. He knocked on the door and entered. The Master Chief Petty Officer, serving as the COB, was sitting at the table with his legs stretched out on the bench. "Master Chief, I need to talk to you."

The Chief made room for the XO to sit, "Come on in, sir, have a seat. What can I do for you?"

"The Commodore has arranged for the crew to get R and R on the island of Corvo. You need to make sure two duty sections get two days off each. We definitely need everyone back on board in four days to finish the refit."

"No problem, sir. The crew will love that news. I suggest you tell them, it'll really make you a big man with them," the old chief responded, grinning from ear to hear.

"Thanks, Master Chief, I'll do that." Bill left, entered the control room, picked up the microphone. "This is the XO, and I have some good news. The boat will be going into port and starboard duty sections. Each section will receive two days on the island just north of here." The crew broke out in cheers though out the boat. When their excitement had subsided, he continued, "Berthing and food will be provided for all hands, but drinks are extra. I wish everyone a good time. Have fun and enjoy yourselves." He hung up the mike and headed to his stateroom.

At 1740, Bill left his cabin and locked the door. He was wearing his dress white uniform, and carrying an overnight bag. He took a couple steps to the Captain's cabin, knocked on the door and asked, "Captain, you ready?"

Almost immediately, Helen opened the door in her dress-white skirt uniform, "Ready, Bill." She picked up a small travel bag. She turned back to Bill. "We better get going, the Commodore doesn't like to be kept waiting."

"Aye, aye, my Captain." Bill smiled, took a step backwards to allow Helen to lead. She pressed by and headed to the control room, which was temporarily empty while the watch was touring the boat. Helen started up the ladder first, paused and looked down at Bill, "I know why you wanted me to go first. You wanted to look up my skirt, you devil." She gave a little laugh and continued up.

Helen's comment caught Bill by surprise. He took a step back so as to not be tempted to, indeed, look. Instead he glanced down the corridor toward his cabin and when Helen disappeared through the hatch above, he stepped onto the ladder and looked up to make sure the way was clear. He saw Helen climbing out the side hatch of the sail and once she was clear, he followed.

Helen was waiting for him. "You realize this is R and R for us too, don't you?"

"As close as we're going to get, anyway," Bill replied.

"Then lighten up. Or are all you brain people sticks-in-the-mud?"

"I'll try to be more fun once we reach Santa Cruz."

"Okay, then. If you improve your behavior, I'll buy the drinks tonight." Helen smiled, as she led the way to the Commodore's stateroom.

As they started up the last flight of stairs the Commodore was coming down. "Hold it right there, you two. Take it the other way, my gig's on the port side." Helen backed down the stairs, waited for the Commodore to pass, then followed him down to the main deck and out a hatch to the weather deck. They proceeded aft to the ladder, then down to the waiting boat. When all three were settled in, the Commodore ordered, "Quartermaster, cast off. Take us to Santa Cruz and don't spare the horses."

"Yes, sir," he replied as he instructed the seaman with him to cast off the lines. The small boat drifted away from the massive ship, as the Quartermaster eased the throttle forward and the boat began to speed toward Santa Cruz. Helen glanced back at the Hunley and the boats tied alongside, bearing members of the Hunley's crew.

Later on Santa Cruz

The small boat pulled along the pier and tied up. "Our accommodations are over there," the Commodore said as he pointed at a two-story building at the end of the pier. The threesome climbed out of the boat and headed toward the building. "I hope you two will be my guests at dinner tonight."

"I think we can manage that, don't you Bill?" Helen responded.

"I don't have any other plans," Bill replied.

"Good, let's get checked in and freshen up. I'll meet you in the dining room in, shall we say, an hour. And wear civilian clothes," the Commodore ordered.

"Yes, sir." Helen and Bill replied. The two slowed to let the Commodore precede them by a few feet. Helen whispered to Bill, "Did you bring civilian clothes?"

"A shirt and a pair of shorts. I hope they'll be okay."

"Sounds like what I brought. Oh well, what do we have to lose?"

An hour later

Helen stepped out of her room, wearing a pair of cut-off shorts and a loose-fitting tank top and walked the short distance along the balcony to Bill's room. She knocked on the door and waited for him to answer. After a brief interval, he opened the door also in cut-offs and a tight-fitting muscle shirt. "Hi Helen, I thought I was stopping by your room."

"I'm getting hungry and tired of waiting, so I came for you. Ready?"

"Let me get my wallet and I will be." Bill turned and reentered his room, leaving Helen at the door. She carefully watched how Bill's shorts fit him.

"Very nice", she thought to herself as Bill bent over, picked up his uniform trousers and removed his wallet from the back pocket. He then tossed them onto the bed. As he turned toward the door, he noticed Helen checking him out and smiled as he walked to her. He exited the room and shut the door behind him. He looked Helen in the eye, "Lead the way, it's my turn to check you out."

Helen strolled along the balcony toward the stairs, putting a little more sway in her walk than normal. She turned into the hallway that concealed the stairs, looked over her shoulder and smiled, "Everything alright back there?"

"Everything looks to be working perfectly from this angle," Bill replied. As they hurried down the stairs, Bill continued, "Helen, this is like I'm back in high school."

"I know what you mean. I feel that way, too." Helen responded as they moved through the door into the lobby. "Now, let's behave before we get in trouble with the Commodore."

Entering the dinning room they saw the Commodore already at a table in the corner. They were surprised he was still in his uniform. They looked questioningly at each other as they crossed to his table. The Commodore stood as they approached. "I'm sorry I won't be able to dine with you tonight," he said apologetically. "Unfortunately I've been called to headquarters, so you two enjoy yourselves. And the meal and drinks are on me. I'll pick you up at 0700 tomorrow."

"You don't have to treat us, sir," Helen stated.

"I know. But I invited you to join me, so I will pay for it even though I won't be here. So, we'll hear no more about it, young lady."

"Yes, sir," Helen replied, sheepishly, as the Commodore picked up his hat off the table and headed for the door.

Bill pulled out a chair for Helen to sit in, then eased around the table and sat opposite her as the waiter strolled up and handed them menus. "Would you care to order an appetizer or drinks," he asked, his voice sporting a soft Spanish accent.

Bill looked at Helen, "What would you like to drink?"

"How about margaritas?"

"Whatever you say. Two margaritas, my good man." Bill told the waiter.

"Very well, two margaritas, I'll be back with your drinks momentarily," the waiter left.

"So, let's see what looks good to eat," Helen said as she opened the menu. Her eyes scrolled down the list until they locked on an item that made her mouth water, "That's it, seafood festival! How about you, you a seafood lover?" She asked Bill.

"Let's just say I rarely turn it down," Bill replied.

The waiter returned after a few minutes with their drinks and Bill ordered the seafood festival for both of them. They spent the next hour eating and downing more margaritas. When they were finished,

Joel M. Fulgham

Helen asked Bill if he wanted to hit another bar since the evening was still young. Bill agreed, reminding Helen that she had offered to buy the drinks. They obtained the waiter's recommendation and left for the suggested bar.

They walked down a deserted beach for about a mile until they came to the place they were seeking. From outside, it looked like a run-down shack on the beach, but the loud rock music and light coming through the open windows betrayed the appearance. As the two grew closer, they saw people dancing past the windows. Coming closer, they located the wooden steps from the beach onto the bar's porch. Standing at the bottom of the stairs, Helen and Bill carefully looked them over before heading up. "Hmm, I guess they'll support us," Bill said.

"Maybe, but what do we have to lose, it won't be too far of a drop if they don't." Helen replied. They headed up the steps.

Entering, they headed directly toward two empty stools at the bar. "You up for another margarita, Number One," Helen asked, smiling. Bill looked at her, confused. "Didn't you ever watch Star Trek as a kid?" Helen added.

"Oh, now I get it," Bill replied with a chuckle. "Captain Picard called Riker that. Sure, more margaritas but why not speed up the process a little bit. Bartender," Bill beckoned to the young woman behind the bar. She came over and Bill ordered two margaritas plus two shots of Jose Gold.

"Are you trying to get me drunk?" Helen asked, a twinkle in her eye.

"Goodness, would I do that to you, My Captain? But you know, now that you mention it, why not?" Bill responded as the bartender sat their drinks on the bar.

Helen picked up her shot and looked at it as she replied, "Okay, but I should warn you, this stuff can make me real downright friendly." Bill picked up his shot, the two toasted each other and downed the warm liquid that burned on its way down. Helen quickly took a sip of her margarita as Bill looked on and laughed. "What's your problem, little girl? I thought you could handle this."

"I can, it's just that the first one always burns on the way down. I bet I know something you can't handle."

World War III
The Beginning

"What might that be?" Bill asked.

"Can you dance to this music?"

"I prefer slow music, but yes, I can dance to this."

"Prove it," Helen teased, as she pulled Bill onto the dance floor where she exhibited her best dirty dancing. It was all Bill could do to keep up with her. Finally, he managed to catch the DJ's attention and motioned for a slow song. The DJ nodded.

The song ended and a slower piece began. Bill looked at Helen sensually, "Now its my turn." He wrapped his arms around her waist and pulled her tightly against him. She, in turn, encircled his neck with her arms and laid her head against his shoulder. They began a sexually rhythmic movement to the music's beat. Helen raised her head up and stared deeply into Bill's eyes. The surroundings faded away as the music took them to a mystical world where only they existed.

Bill kissed her, slowly and softly at first, but then his kisses grew in passion as she returned them. Suddenly, the music stopped and they were abruptly brought back to reality by the cheers of the people around them. They looked around at the onlookers and blushed. Bill cleared his throat and whispered, "I think we should finish our drinks and get out of here."

Helen continued to look around and finally replied, "Maybe we should just leave now."

"If that's okay with you, let's go." He took her by the hand and led her out the door, down the stairs to the beach to the fading applause from the patrons.

On the beach, they walked slowly with their arms around each other, towards their hotel. Once out of sight of the bar, Helen stopped and asked, "You up for a late night swim?"

Bill glanced up and down the beach before answering, "Sure, why not." He quickly pulled his shirt over his head, then off came his shoes. Then, to Helen's surprise, he unfastened his shorts and let them fall to the sand. Finally, he hooked his thumbs inside his briefs and slowly pulled them down, stood up straight and looked directly into her eyes, "Well, I'm ready, what are you waiting for?"

"Just enjoying the scenery," She replied.

"Has anyone ever told you you're a devil?"

"Not in several years." Helen grasped the bottom of her shirt and slowly pulled it up to her neck, teasing him as stripper would. She smiled briefly, spun away from him as she yanked it over her head and dropped it to the ground. She then unfastened her shorts and wriggled out of them, letting them plop to the ground. She covered her breasts with her arms as she turned back to Bill, "Okay, I'm ready to go in."

Bill looked down at her underwear, shook his head disapprovingly, "No way, everything has got to go."

"You sure?" She responded coyly.

"Yes, ma'am, positive."

She turned again, removed her panties and as soon as they were on the ground, made a mad dash for the water. Bill was temporarily caught off guard by Helen, but quickly recovered and took off after her. He was able to catch her in the rough surf as they fell into the water. When they surfaced they were locked in a passionate embrace as they explored each other's bodies. In a flash, they were consumed by each other as their passion was urgently aroused and they were soon aware only of the other.

0630 the next morning

Helen emerged from her room in her dress white uniform and walked to Bill's room. She knocked on the door and Bill answered, also in his dress whites. Helen quickly darted through the open doorway and threw her arms around Bill's neck, giving him a long, passionate kiss. Bill responded, wrapped his arms tightly around her waist. When they finally parted, he suggested they get downstairs for breakfast, so as to meet the Commodore at 0700 hours. They casually walked along the balcony, hiding the feelings of moments before. They were well aware of the trouble their new relationship could cause their careers. When they reached the dining room, the Commodore was seated at a table to one side of the room and motioned the two officers to join him.

The three enjoyed the best breakfast they had had in weeks, a pleasant change from shipboard food. The three chatted idly, careful not to mention the upcoming meeting, for spies could be anywhere. Finally, the Commodore after a glance at his watch, said, "We'd better be on our way. It's not a good idea to keep Admirals and Generals waiting."

They strolled out and got into the waiting Hummer. On the drive Helen and Bill were fascinated by the lovely gardens they passed. Soon, they pulled in front of a concrete-block building, surrounded by armed Marines and anti-aircraft batteries.

They dismounted the vehicle and walked toward the building with the Commodore leading. As they approached the Marines, the Sergeant in charge snapped to attention and saluted. The Commodore returned the salute and the Sergeant queried, "May I see your identification, please?"

The three showed their military IDs to the Sergeant, who checked them and saluted again. "They're about ready to began. Please step inside, then go down the stairs to the left."

"Thank you, Sergeant." The Commodore replied, as they entered the building, went down the stairway three flights, through two steel doors and into a large meeting room with a huge wooded table. The walls were covered maps of the various battle theatres. Some showed fine details of military installations, and some were of areas with troop locations and types indicated by pins.

Several people were gathered around a small table in the corner, on which were a coffee pot and cups. Alongside was a refrigerator labeled, sodas and juices. Admiral Schmidt sat at the far end of the table, sipping from a cup while looking through a stack of papers. As the newcomers entered the room, he stood and cleared his throat to get the attention of the others in the room. "Ladies and gentleman, the spearhead of our plan has finally arrived. Now we can start the meeting. Commodore, please, I'd like you three to sit at this end of the table." They went to where Steve motioned and Helen took the chair to the right of the Admiral and Bill sat at his left. The Commodore took the chair next to Helen.

Once everyone was seated, Steve began, "The first order of business is to congratulate the Hunley on a job well done." The people around the table applauded briefly. "Captain St. Johns and Commander Floyd, without the efforts of you and your crew, the first battle would have been a complete defeat. We would certainly have lost the Med fleet and the Republic would still have those two carriers and a few more escort vessels. Thank you for your performance above and beyond the call of duty." Another round of applause filled the room. "Every member of the crew will receive a commendation. For the next order of business, Secretary of State, Jenny Watson will update everyone on the Republic's status." He looked to the far end of the table and held out his hand, "Madam Secretary."

Jenny rose and walked to a chart on the wall and pointed at Japan, which was covered by a red dot. "The main island of Japan fell to the Republic yesterday and bombings has reduced their manufacturing capacity to almost nothing. The Republic's invasion fleet has stayed close to Japan and not moved to attack anywhere else. Israel, as you already know, has been lost. Spain and Portugal are also totally under the control of the Republic. Recon shows they're continuing to build up troop strength in, both the Atlantic and Med. Possibly in preparation for an invasion of France, Great Britain, or both. Italy has been invaded and the enemy has moved as far north as Rome, where the Italian army and Air Force have managed to halt their advance. However, satellites indicate another flotilla forming in Tripoli, which our analysts think, could be for a landing north of Rome. Greece has experienced bombings but no invasion, as yet. The Republic planes sent against England and France have been turned back and on the eastern front, Turkey is still neutral and so no aggressive moves have been made toward it or Russia. Any Questions?"

"Yes, ma'am," General Glassgold spoke up. "Have we notified the Italians that they must prepare for a northern invasion?"

"No, sir."

"May I ask why?"

"We feel the Republic may be unaware we've launched our satellites. What we've been observing shows they're not trying to hide anything. If we pass on this information, it will tip our hand."

"Beggin' your pardon, Ma'am, but are we to sit by and watch the rest of the world be taken over by them?" the General retorted.

"If you'll just bear with me, you'll hear our plan," Jenny replied, maintaining her calm appearance. "Are there any other questions?" No one spoke. "Very well, Admiral, your turn."

"Thank you Madam Secretary. The main operation, code-named 'Intruder', will be a two-step process. The Hunley will leave here in five days, carrying a strike force of SEALs." He walked to a map of the Med. "She'll make best possible speed to a point off the west coast of Morocco where the SEALs will disembark. The Hunley will then make a high-speed run through the straits and take up a station here…" He pointed to an area between Tripoli and Italy. And will sink as many enemy ships as possible. Our analyst suggests that the Republic's flotilla will be assembled and ready to deploy in about seven days. We hope the Hunley will make the Republic think an old-style wolf pack is in the Med. If so, they may withdraw some front line forces to find and destroy the threat. If this occurs, we'll move our carriers into range of their fleet and engage them. We've cleared Norfolk, sinking the enemy submarine deployed there, so five of our submarines from there are currently en route to join our carriers. We've been unable to find the Republic's third submarine, so Jacksonville is still considered blocked. While our fleet engages theirs, aircraft from England, France and Germany will attack the Republic's bases in Spain. With luck, splitting their forces will give us the edge we need to stop their advance dead in its tracks. Remember, the main focus of this engagement is to prevent a landing in Northern Italy and inflict maximum damage on the enemy forces in Spain. If the naval engagement goes bad, Admiral Mora will immediately disengage. We can't afford to lose many more ships at this point. Once the SEALs have accomplished their mission, they will contact the Hunley to pick them up at a location to be determined. Are there anymore questions?"

"Yes, Admiral," Helen spoke up. "You know, when we engaged the battleship in the straits, we also encountered a mine field. How do we avoid that?"

"Oh, I forgot, sorry. We've had a team from the Seawolf mapping the area since your report. Next?"

Admiral Mora chimed in, "What if the Republic fails to pull back their forces?"

Steve drew a deep breath before answering. "In that case, the Hunley will continue attacking enemy ships as long as she can and wait for the SEALs to contact her. The Navy and Air Force will then have to wait to implement plan B. Meanwhile, the stealth bombers and fighters will continue nightly runs against strongholds in Spain."

"Admiral, what are the SEALs going after?" Bill asked.

The Admiral looked over at Jenny who spoke up, "Their mission is classified, on a need to know basis."

"Admiral, what's the targeting priority, warships or transport first?" Helen queried.

"The more combat vessels you sink, the more likely they are to pull back. However, the more transports you take out, the fewer troops they'll have to land in Italy. In short, Commander, the decision is yours, based on what is presented to you and your condition at the moment."

The Admiral looked around the room, waiting for someone else to speak. "Jenny, you have anything else?" She shook her head no. "Then, this meeting is adjourned. Good hunting and God's speed."

Everyone gathered around the coffee pot for small talk before heading back to their commands. The Commodore led Helen and Bill back to the waiting Hummer. They climbed in and sped off to the Hotel. The Commodore turned, looked at them, "We'll be leaving at 1500 hours, so if you want to enjoy the beach and get some sun before we leave, go ahead. However, I'm going souvenir shopping, you want to join me?"

"Thank you Sir, the beach sounds like an excellent idea. I think I'll get some sun while I can," Helen replied, as she glanced over at Bill.

"That sound like a good idea, Captain," Bill added. The Commodore turned forward as Helen gave Bill's leg a quick squeeze.

The Commodore dropped them off and said, "See you at the gig at 1500 hours. Don't be late, we don't want to finish the trip in the dark." He motioned his driver to go.

Helen and Bill headed to their rooms. Walking along the balcony Bill turned to Helen, "See you in about ten minutes?"

"If it'll take you that long to change, then yes," She replied coyly.

"Well then, it's a race. Last one out has to, uh..." Bill started.

"Do whatever the other says, whenever the other wants them to," Helen cut in.

"Okay, you're on." Bill replied as he hurriedly opened the door to his room. Bill rushed into his room and dashed for his travel bag, frantically looking for his shorts and shirt.

Helen stepped into her room and closed the door. She pulled her shirt off, under which she wore a white bikini. She tossed her shirt on the bed, unfastened her skirt and allowed it to drop to the floor. She then kicked off her black pumps, slipped on the sandals lying next to the bed, picked up a towel and stepped outside and waited for Bill.

A few minutes later, he came rushing out of room, still pulling on his shirt. He jumped as Helen cracked, "It's about time, what kept you?"

"How'd you do that?" He stammered.

"I'll never tell." She replied, grinning. "Come on, we're wasting time." She headed down the balcony towards the beach.

Bill took off after her, watching the way she moved. He asked. "Okay. You win. What do I have to do?"

"Don't worry about it now. I'll let you know in due time." She giggled.

"Oh, oh, sounds like trouble." Bill replied nervously. He trailed after her to the beach and after a short walk, Helen spread her towel on the sand amid a large group of people. Bill placed his next to her's and was about to lie down.

"What do you think you're doing?" She said in a demanding voice.

"Get some sun. Why?"

"You're supposed to do whatever I say, remember?"

"Of course I remember, but you said not to worry about it for now. You'd let me know when." Bill rebuffed.

"Well, it's now later, so let's go for swim," she demanded and walked into the water. Bill arose and dutifully followed. When the water reached her shoulders, she turned to see Bill about 20 yards behind.

When he caught up with her he asked, "Okay, where do you want to swim?"

Joel M. Fulgham

"When we're ready, we'll swim back in. But, right now I want is a repeat of last night," she said, handing him something under the water.

Bill lifted the bottom of her swimsuit. "Wow! I'm going to enjoy taking orders from you," Bill said with a smile, as he wrapped his arms around her and pulled her close to him.

Later they swam back to shore, where they both dropped onto their towels, exhausted.

Later, Bill rose up on his elbow and ran his eyes up and down her body as he wondered what he was doing with his Commanding Officer. He finally surrendered the thought, assuring himself that sometimes it's better not to analyze too much.

They relaxed under the sun until two in the afternoon, then walked, silently, back to their rooms, showered and prepared to leave. There was a knock on Bill's door. He opened it and Helen entered. She held her gaze down as she spoke, "Bill, what are we getting into?"

Bill placed his finger under her chin and lifted her head so their eyes met. "Whatever it is, I don't care. I'm happy with it."

As he finished, she fell into his arms and whispered, "I love you." They stood there, in an embrace for several minutes before heading off to meet the Commodore. The ride home was awkward and quiet, with the conversation dominated by the Commodore as he talked of the plans ahead.

Chapter 13

Back on board the Hunley

"Eng, how are the repairs going?"

"Repairs to the periscopes will be completed tomorrow, seawater system repairs are about fifty percent complete and electrical work is well underway. In two more days the testing can start. Work on the Conn is going well, torpedo room repairs are about completed and we're loading torpedoes tomorrow. The divers have finished checking the hull and made some minor repairs. And, people from the XO's design team have been here, and talked to members of the crew about the boat's performance and took measurements."

"Took measurements, of what?" She asked.

"The control room, engineering, crawl ways, etcetera."

Helen thought for a minute, "Go ask the XO to come here."

"Sure," the Eng left and in a few seconds Bill and the Eng entered.

"Bill, have you any idea why people from your design team have been checking out the Hunley?"

"Checking it out, how?" he responded.

"Taking measurements of different areas."

"They may be here to calculate how to improve the high-speed handling."

"Would they need to measure the dive and helm for that?" queried Mr. Mackie.

"The dive and helm? Maybe they've solved the software-hardware interface problem with the computer control system." Bill replied.

"What computer control system?" Helen asked.

"The original design called for an advanced control system for navigation and depth control. A computer would control all operations, and the system would have had an absolute override switch with a positive disconnect for manual control in case of malfunction. However, we couldn't get the bugs worked out, so we went with the conventional control systems," Bill explained. "If that's

Joel M. Fulgham

it, they're simply verifying what is actually here against the drawings, so they can design the new panels."

"Sounds like a major undertaking, removing what we have and installing this new system," the Eng suggested.

"We think it can be accomplished in two months." Bill informed him.

"Okay, then we won't have to worry about it for a while," Helen cut in. "What we do have to worry about is getting the boat ready for combat and we won't have the full crew back for three more days. If the tender people can keep at the repairs, we should finish two or three days at the most, that will give us time to test everything and fix any problems we find. We also have to replenish our stores and make room for our passengers. Eng, go ahead and test the systems as they're repaired. I'd like start a precrit and reactor startup as soon as the electrical work is done. Any questions?"

"No, ma'am."

"Okay, thank you." Helen dismissed him and motioned Bill to stay. "Have you figured out where our guests will stay?"

"Most will stay in the torpedo room and crew's lounge. Their commander can use my room and I'll stay in here." Helen shot him a look that said, you've got to be kidding. Then he continued, "I can sleep in the ward room for the one night they'll be on board. It won't be real comfortable for anyone, but we'll get through it."

"Good. The Commodore said the SEALs would bring their gear aboard tomorrow."

"Damn it! I forgot about the gear. I guess that'll have to go into the library."

"How could you forget about something so simple," Helen asked.

Bill looked into her blue eyes for a moment before answering, "I guess I've been a little preoccupied."

"Is there something I can do to help?" she replied with a devilish grin.

"No, I don't think so. You see, I met this girl on the island and I'm having trouble getting her out of my head."

"Maybe you could stop in later and we can discuss it." She brushed her hand against his leg.

Bill smiled at her. "I think I can arrange to be available around, say 2300 hours. Will the door be open?"

"Wide open," she replied as she stood up and gave him a kiss on the cheek. "But for now I think you should check out the rest of the boat."

Bill smiled at her, "Aye, aye, mon Capitaine." He turned and left her standing there.

Tripoli, Meeting room below the Royal Palace.

General Kadala remained in the safety of his underground quarters since the attack on Libya. He now gathered his top advisors to update him on the status of the war.

"General, the invasion of Europe is continuing as scheduled. Once the next wave lands in Northern Italy, we will control the entire northern coast of the Mediterranean. Our navy, though, has taken a beating. The Americans have developed a new type of submarine that we have been unable to detect. It sneaks up close to our ships and fires torpedoes before we know it's there. The only thing that betrays her location is when she fires them."

"What do you suggest we do, Admiral?" Kadala asked, turning to the little man sitting to his right.

The Admiral of the Islamic fleet shifted nervously in his chair. "All we can do is inform our fleet of this new threat. In the notice we should advise them to continually listen for her firing torpedoes and be ready to launch their counter measures and anti-submarine weapons into the area from which the torpedoes came."

"Is that the best you can do?" Kadala shot back.

"Until we can figure out another way to detect it, yes it is," he emphatically replied.

Kadala leaned back in his chair and thought for a moment. "Very well, if that's the best we can do, inform the fleet. Now, is there any other earth-shattering news?" Kadala paused, waiting for a reply that never came. "I think it's time for us to let the Americans know how serious we are. Inform our agents to proceed with their next objective."

Joel M. Fulgham

USS Hunley

Bill finished his trip through the boat and he checked his watch as he slowly walked to the forward compartments. He thought pleasantly about what awaited him, for had been a long time since he felt this way about anyone. His thoughts drifted back to his last involvement. She was a lot like Helen, especially her eyes. So, maybe that's what it's really about-the all-caring loving eyes. The horror of the day it ended returned. Why had he been so stupid? He knew he had too much to drink and should not have been driving. He should be the one in a grave, not her.

Bill's reverie was interrupted by someone calling to him, "XO, excuse me Sir." Bill turned to see Fireman Johnson. "The Eng would like to see you in maneuvering."

"Thank you, Johnson," he replied as he headed back to see the Eng. Bill knocked on the side of maneuvering's enclosure and pulled the curtain back, "Hey Eng, you wanted to see me?"

"Yes, sir, come in. I want to give you some good news. The impulse drive system is finally back to full operating condition."

"Thanks. That's about the best news I've heard. The Captain will be glad to hear it, too. I'm on my way to fill her in on what I saw throughout the boat."

"While you're here, can I ask what's up?"

"You can ask, but I can't tell you. That's up to the captain. What I can tell you though is that the crew's library will be off limits, starting tomorrow."

"Okay, if that's all you can tell me." Bill turned to leave. "Hey XO, glad to have you two back. Now I can concentrate on getting this thing put back together again."

"I thought you were suppose to go on R&R?"

"Not at this time, my life depends on these repairs and I'd rather be here to make sure they're done right"

"Okay, it's good to be back. You make sure you have this lady ready on time, and I'll try to keep the other lady out of your hair." The two men laughed. Bill left the Eng to do his thing.

A few minutes later, Bill entered his cabin, closed and locked the door. He opened his small closet, reached inside and pulled out his robe and shower bag. He tossed them on his bunk, removed his shoes,

World War III
The Beginning

unzipped his jumpsuit and climbed out of it. He entered the head. He stepped inside the shower. Over the sound of the water, he heard Helen's door open. The shower door opened, to reveal a naked Helen smiling at him. Slowly she stepped into the shower, putting an arm around Bill's neck and closed the door behind her. Helen pulled him to her as Bill playfully resisted and whispered, "Captain, I'm glad to see you. Mackie informed me that the impulse drive is now completely operational."

"That's nice," she replied. "Do you have anything else for me?"

He gave an expression of deep thought for a moment, "Well, now that you mention it, there is this other matter," He replied as he put his arms around her waist, and pulled her tight against him as they kissed.

Chapter 14

The Next Morning

Bill and Helen were snuggled in Bill's bunk when there's a knock on the door. "Just a minute." He rolled over and kisses Helen, trying to wake her so she wouldn't make a noise. She responded by throwing an arm around his neck and returning the kiss. He placed a finger across her lips and whispered, "Someone's at the door. You need to get out of here." Startled, she kisses him and rolled out of bed, making her getaway through the head. Bill watched her leave, then struggled out of the bunk, and slipped on his robe. He opened the door to see Fireman Johnson waiting patiently. "Yes Johnson, what's up?"

"Excuse me sir, but there's a Commander Adamowicz waiting to see you in the wardroom."

Bill looked at her, puzzled, and then surmised Adamowicz must be the SEAL's commander. "Thank you, tell him I'll be there in a moment."

"Yes, sir," she replied as she turned and headed back to the wardroom.

Bill closed the door, picked up his pants and stepped into the head. He knocked softly on Helen's door and waited for her reply, then entered her cabin. "Commander Adamowicz is waiting for me in the wardroom," he informed her.

"Is he with the SEALS?"

"I think so," Bill replied. "I'll know for sure in a few minutes. You want to meet him?"

"No, you go ahead and show him around. I'll catch up."

"Yes, ma'am," Bill went back to his cabin, finished dressing, then left his room.

A few minutes later he entered the wardroom and the two men greeted each other with a strong handshake. "Commander, would you care for a cup of coffee before I show you around?"

Adamowicz looked Bill sternly in the eyes and replied, "No thanks, I have work to do and I've been held up long enough waiting on you. I would like to skip the pleasantries and see where my men can store their gear."

World War III
The Beginning

Bill was stunned and momentarily at a loss for words. He studied the man as he gathered his thoughts and formulated a reply. "Look mister, you better back up and chill out. This sub ain't big enough for a chip on anyone's shoulder. Now, I'm going to get myself a cup of coffee and after I drink it, I will show you where to stow your gear. Understand?" Bill turned and headed for the galley. Where he stuck his head through the door and asked the cook for coffee. The young seaman filled a cup. As he handed it to Bill, he whispered, "What an asshole."

Bill smiled, "I'll say, but if he keeps it up, I'll put a cork in it." The seaman laughed softly and returned to his work.

Bill turned and stared at the man before him. Then, in an act of defiance, he leaned against the doorway and took a sip from the cup. Without taking his eyes off of Adamowicz, Bill spoke to the Seaman in the galley, "Man, this has to be the best cup of coffee I ever tasted. My compliments to the person who made this." Bill finally spoke again to the Commander, "This is really good, are you sure you don't want any?" Bill took another sip as he waited for a reply.

"No, sir. I just want to know where my men can stow their gear."

"Hold your horses." Bill turned to the galley, "Jacobs, freshen this up, please." The seaman brought a pot of coffee to the doorway and filled Bill's cup. Bill turned and started toward the door to the passageway, "Alright, follow me Adamowicz." Bill led through the passageway, down a ladder to the crew's lounge, then into the library. "This is it. Big enough?"

"I think we can fit everything in here." The man replied in an almost uncivil tone.

Bill ignored the slight. "Now, for the sleeping arrangements, some of your men will have to sleep in here," he said as they walked back into the crew's lounge. "Most will have to sleep in the torpedo room. If we need more room, some can bed down in the bow compartment. You'll sleep in my cabin."

The commander interrupted at this, "That won't be necessary, I'll share sleeping arrangements with my men."

"Very well, if that's what you want. It works for me."

"Now," Adamowicz said, "If you don't mind, I'll get my men started bringing the gear down and stowing it. I'll post a guard at the library door to make sure no one bothers the equipment." He waited for Bill to reply before turning to leave.

"No problem, do what you have to do. But remember, every member of this crew has a secret clearance, which means they can be trusted," Bill retorted.

The SEAL Commander stared into Bill's eyes and snapped, "My mission is classified top secret, so your crew shouldn't even know we're here. But, I guess some things can't be helped." Mouthing this final insult, he turned and made his way off the boat.

Bill watched him leave, then mumbled, "That man's a real sweetheart." He then headed to Helen's cabin.

On his way, Jacobs stopped him, "XO, may I say that, watching you put that SEAL in his place was absolutely great. I feel I'm in the presence of a master."

Bill smiled at the young man, "Thank you Jacobs, but let's keep this between the two of us, okay."

"If that's your wish, sir. But the rest of the crew would sure love to hear about it."

"After this mission, maybe." Bill headed up the ladder. When he arrived at Helen's cabin, he knocked and waited before opening the door. Upon receiving permission, he entered and told her about how much of an ass the SEAL's leader was. Helen laughed heartily when he also told her of the cook's reaction to how he'd handled the Commander. The story told, they got down to planning for getting the boat ready for sea. They still had a few major repairs to complete plus loading of a fresh supply of torpedoes, food and repair parts.

As the two were going over their plan, the Weapons Officer interrupted with a knock on the door. "Excuse me, Captain. We're ready to load torpedoes and await your safety inspection."

Helen said she'd be there in a few seconds, then looked at the list and handed it to Bill, instructing him to go over it with the Engineering Officer. Bill took it and headed aft. Helen headed to the torpedo room.

As Helen entered, the Weapons Officer handed her a clipboard. "Okay," she said, "Let's see the machinery operate."

World War III
The Beginning

Petty Officer Casey faced the control panel and pushed the button that started the loading skid. It moved along tracks in the floor until it reached the turntable, whereupon Casey released the button. He threw a switch that made the table turn 90 degrees, then pushed the table-controller button again and the table rolled to the stop at the end of the track. Casey flipped another switch, which raised the table to the top storage rack. He then moved to the end of the storage rack and pulled a pin, which held a lever in position. The man then pushed the lever to the right and watched long forks with concave grooves the size of a torpedo, emerge from the racks and slide under where a torpedo would be on the table. With them in position he pushed the up lever and lifted the imaginary torpedo off the table and retracted the forks into position.

At this point Helen interrupted and said she was satisfied with the operation of the equipment. She walked to the sound powered-phone and contacted maneuvering. "Maneuvering, this is the Captain. I need you to verify the pressure in the vital hydraulic system and that all three pumps are in auto. Make your report to me in the control room."

"Verify the vital hydraulic system pressure and that all three pumps are operating, aye, Captain," came from the voice on the other end. Helen replaced the handset and turned toward the Weapons Officer, "Shall we go topside?"

"Lead the way, Ma'am." Helen headed topside via the Control room. As the two officers entered the control room, the Duty Officer was on the phone and said, "Wait one, the Captain just came in." She turned to the Captain, "Captain, Maneuvering wants to talk to you."

Helen walked onto the conn and picked up the phone, "This is the Captain."

"Captain, this is Maneuvering. Vital hydraulic system pressure is 3000 pounds. Pumps one, two and three are in auto."

Helen responded, "Very well," and marked it off on her check sheet. She then climbed up the ladder to the sail. The Weapons Officer followed her. Once topside, they inspected the ramp leading down to the torpedo room. Helen had several crewman grab the hook that lowers the torpedo down the ramp, pull the line out as the winch let it out, then fed the line back as the winch was reversed. Helen signed off, but the final requirement was for her to go up to the crane supervisor on the Cable and she dashed up the long ladder that extended up the side of the massive ship alongside. She walked aft, through a passageway until she reached the next ladder. It led up three decks to the crane deck. Then out another hatch and forward to where a group of sailors were gathered, waiting to transfer the torpedoes to the submarine.

The senior Petty Officer stepped forward and greeted her with a salute. Helen returned the salute and asked for the crane supervisor. He replied that he was and she asked to see his daily checklist. The Petty Officer First Class flipped through the pages on his clipboard until he found what he was looking for and handed it to Helen. Helen scanned it and thanked him. She signed off on the last line as she headed back the way she'd come.

The Petty Officer watched her leave as he backed toward his crane crew. One man walked up behind him and jabbed him in the ribs with his finger and joked, "What do you think you're looking at Mickey? She's your superior officer?"

Not taking his eyes off Helen, he replied, "Yes, but wouldn't you like to serve under her?"

The other men laughed and one said, "Come on, stud, let's start moving these things."

Helen disappeared around the corner and the man finally turned around, walked to the drop hatch to the torpedo storeroom and called down, "You ready to pull it yet?"

Another Petty Officer appeared at the bottom of the hatch, "It's about time! We've been waiting on you! Take it away!"

The supervisor held up his right hand, fingers pointing up toward the crane operator and tapped his fingers together. The operator slowly brought up the object he, himself, could not see. The torpedo left it's cart below and the supervisor rotated his raised index finger, meaning to bring it up at normal speed. Once the torpedo cleared the hatch and hung about ten feet above the deck, he signaled the operator to stop, by holding up his fist. The deck crew then swung the torpedo over the side and it began it' decent to the submarine.

Helen arrived at the bottom of the ladder, just as her crew was positioning the deadly object onto the ramp. She stopped at the bottom of the ladder and watched. The crane operator slowly lowered his load until it rested on the ramp, but most of the weight was still held by the crane. The sub's topside crew connected their winch cable to the end of the torpedo, then signaled for the crane to ease its tension. They removed the crane's lifting fixture and sent it back up for the next torpedo. The sub's winch slowly let the torpedo slide down the rollers on the ramp toward the torpedo room. Once it disappeared below the deck, Helen walked toward the ramp and looked down it, then at the young men and women involved in the action. "Excellent job, keep up the good work and we'll finish ahead of schedule." Then she disappeared through the side hatch on the sail.

Chapter 15

Midnight at a small field in Cuba

Two men strolled past several dilapidated old buildings. The weather they'd been awaiting had arrived. The sky was heavily overcast and the night pitch black. Suddenly large doors opened in the side of the buildings, revealing modern aircraft hangers. Each held three, fully-armed, solid-black, attack helicopters.

The ground crews were hooking small tractors to the front of each, to extract them from their nests. As the copters emerged from their hangers, their huge blades fanned out and locked in flight position. Each, in turn, started its engines and prepared to take off into the night.

The pilots ran through their preflight checks as they were tugged to their take-off positions of two groups, each forming a delta attack formation. The tractors were disconnected and moved out of the way as the first group revved it engines, and rolled a few yards and took off as one. Once airborne, they kicked in the jet propulsion units and flew off to the north. Once the formation reached the ocean they dropped to an altitude of fifty feet above the water to avoid radar contact as long as possible. The second formation departed a few minutes later, following the same flight path.

0130 Homestead Airforce Base

The control tower was bathed in an eerie, green light emitted from the radar screens and was designed for a crew of ten controllers and one Operations Officer. Due to downsizing the military, it was now manned during daytime hours by four controllers and an Officer. At night there were only two controllers and an Officer. This night, one of the controllers sat at his monitor, puzzled.

He called the Operations Officer over.

"Yes, Sergeant, what you got," The older man walked up behind the operator and laid a hand on his shoulder.

"Captain, I saw three blips at the southern end of the radar's range on my screen for a second, but they vanished."

"Well, let me know if you see them again." He turned and walked briskly back to his desk in the center of the room, sat down, picked up his phone and dialed the Flight Commander. In a few seconds the phone is answered by a deep voice, "Flight Commander."

"Sir, this is Operations. One of our operators saw three blips on his screen that disappeared right away. I suggest we scramble on interceptor to investigate?"

"No, I don't think so. Call Sinbad and Cowboy and have them fly down to investigate." replied an apparently unconcerned voice.

"Yes Sir, but a flyby is all they'd be able to do, They'll be very low on fuel by then." The Operation Officer answered.

"Well, I think a flyby's all that's required. It was probably a false echo."

"Very well, Sir, will do." He hung up and called to the Sergeant. "Sergeant, have Sinbad and Cowboy check the area before they return to base."

"Yes, Sir." The young man contacted the planes and gave them the heading that would take them into the area of the unidentified contacts. "Captain, the planes are en route, ETA thirty minutes."

The men continued their jobs for another twenty minutes when the three contacts reappeared on the screen. "Captain Roberts, the contacts are back, five miles out and closing fast!"

"Damn it!" Roberts shouted. "Contact Sinbad, have him get back here ASAP!" As he finished the order, he picked up the phone and quickly buzzed the Flight Commander to inform him of the situation.

"Sound the air raid siren! Scramble the standby fighters. I'll inform the Base Commander."

Roberts ran to the wall and hit the air raid button. He then picked up a microphone and ordered the pilots in the ready room to scramble.

As men ran from their barracks to man the anti-aircraft guns, the control tower took a direct hit by a missile. The explosion lit up the field and sent nearby personnel flying through the air. Seconds later, one of the large hangers was hit by another missile, shards of metal and glass sliced through anything or anyone in its path. At the

Joel M. Fulgham

same time, a third missile exploded amid a row of fighters, creating a chain-reaction of explosions through the remaining fighters.

As the attacking helicopters circled for another run, they picked up the two approaching fighters on their radar and split up. Two copters peeled off and went wide for their run while the leader increased his speed and attempted to beat the fighters to the field. He engaged electronic radar-jamming and released foil packs as he lined up on one of the runways. Locking on his target, his warning systems came alive and alerted him that missiles had been fired at him. He launched his missile, banked hard left and released a flare. The incoming missile locked onto the flare, sped past the helicopter and exploded as it hit the ground. His own missile buried itself in the middle of the runway and detonated, creating a huge crater that would render it unusable for awhile. The helicopter alarm warned of another incoming missile. The pilot shoved the throttle to its stop and steered between two hangers at the edge of the field. As he entered the passageway, the missile smashed into the hanger and destroyed it. The pilot skillfully maneuvered the craft close above the trees, hoping the fighter would lose him. Once clear, he slowed and turned to see where the fighter was and how his companions were doing. He saw only one other helicopter still in the air, with a fighter closing on it. He watched in silent horror as the fighter launched a missile and the helicopter disappeared. He then saw the two fuel-starved fighters land.

With the fighters down, he had his big chance. He maneuvered close to the trees until he was in range of the airfield. Unhesitatingly, he rose above the trees and shoved the throttle forward. This time though, the base's defenses where ready and the air was immediately filled with anti-aircraft fire. The pilot raced toward the field and locking on the runway, launched his final missiles and turned away dropping as low as he could. Too late! The bullets found their mark just as the missiles found theirs.

The pilot fought the controls as he radioed the three incoming-choppers that his mission was accomplished. Turning his wounded machine toward the Atlantic Ocean, he hoped he could ditch and avoid capture. Nursing the failing engine as long as he possible, the machine finally fell into the water and disappeared.

World War III
The Beginning

With the airbase unusable, the remaining helicopters continued north over the Everglades. Approaching the heavily populated coast of Florida, the bright lights of Miami grew closer, a beacon directing them to their target. They spread out and locked onto the tallest building within their sights, each being a hotel. The helicopters fired their missiles. The buildings exploded, then crashed into the ground. Each helicopter launched six missiles before they turned for home. Miami was in ruins, with a heavy loss of life. Much of the city would continue to burn for days and weeks.

General Wish's house

Mike was sound asleep, having his best sleep since the war started, his wife, Cathy, cuddled up behind him, She was happy to have him home for the first time since the war started. Their sleep was interrupted by the jangle of the phone next to the bed. Mike instantly woke up and picked up the instrument. "Hello."

A somber voice on the other end announced, "General, sorry to wake you, but you need to turn on CNN. Miami has been attacked."

"What! Who?" Mike replied, disbelieving what he heard.

"No, sir," the voice replied, then slowly added, "CNN is reporting the pilots spoke Spanish. Miami International reports the aircraft came in from the South. Also, we've been unable to reach Homestead, to find out why they didn't respond."

Mike fumbled around for the remote as he listened to the voice on the other end of the line. "If you can't reach Homestead, try Miami International for what they know. Contact NAS Jacksonville and have them send a flight to see what's up." While talking, he quit looking for the remote. He rolled out of bed, turned on the TV and sat on the foot of the bed to watch. The picture that unfolded in front of him made him gasp. The destruction was incredible. Then the picture switched to an aerial view of Homestead and Mike dropped the phone in shock. Once he recovered, Mike picked up the phone, "Who are you anyway?" Mike finally asked.

"Oh, sorry, Sir, Captain Fitzsimmons, Air Defense."

"Well Captain, you can forget Homestead. Have Jacksonville send air rescue outfits to Miami, pronto. Contact Andrews and have them alert the other Joint Chiefs to rendezvous there in one hour. And send a helicopter to Arlington to pick me up. Tell them the code word is Cyclops. You got that?"

"Yes Sir, will do." The phone clicked.

Cathy sat up beside him and wrapped her arms around his neck as she looked at the TV screen. "Who could have done this?" she asked softly.

Mike slowly turned to look at her, "Probably Cuba." He answered, still in a state of disbelief.

Kadala's Bunker

Kadala sat at his desk when the Minister of Defense barged in, shouting, "General, they did it! Our agents report total success. Miami is burning, Homestead is out of action and CNN is reporting Cuba responsible for the attack."

"Very good Minister. Congratulations on a job well done. Now the Americans will pull back some of their fleet and aircraft to protect against another attack from their little neighbor to the south, or maybe they'll even invade Cuba. Send my congratulations to all involved."

Chapter 16

USS Hunley

"Station the Maneuvering Watch," came over the speakers from Helen, on the bridge about to cast off.

The speaker came alive, "Captain, all stations report manned and ready."

Helen spoke into the mike, "Very well," then called out to the crewmembers on deck, "Cast off all lines." In unison the hawsers were undone and thrown off and the boat began to drift away from the tender. Helen spoke into the intercom, "Ahead slow."

Slowly the boat inched forward as the drive transducers became charged. Once clear of the tender, Helen ordered ahead full. The boat gained speed and soon left the huge tender behind. "Flood maneuvering tanks," Helen ordered over the intercom. The submarines hull slowly sank below the surface of the water. Only the sail remained above. Helen glanced back at the tender, then ordered the lookouts to clear the bridge and for Bill to wait in his cabin. Helen followed the lookouts down the hatch, closing each hatch as she went. At the bottom of the ladder, she ordered the Diving Officer to take the boat down to 300 feet. "Dive, Dive," echoed throughout the craft followed by the blare of the klaxon. The Chief of the Watch checked his board and announced it was green. "Open all main ballast tank vents," the Dive continued.

As the boat descended, Helen spoke again, "Quartermaster, give me a heading for check point Igloo."

"Yes Ma'am, wait one," she replied as she moved equipment around the charts. "Captain, new heading should be one-hundred-twenty-eight degrees."

"Very well. Dive, come right to new heading one-hundred-twenty-eight, ahead flank," Helen ordered.

Before the Diving Officer could execute the order, Ensign Crockett interrupted, "Excuse me Captain, but that heading will take us very close to the Republic's fleet."

Helen looked at her for a second before replying, "Very good, Ensign, you were listening. Dive, come right to heading one-six-five degrees, ahead flank."

"Heading one-six-five, ahead flank, aye," the Dive repeated.

Then Helen looked at the Quartermaster and asked, "Why didn't you pick up on that?"

"I try not to question your orders, Captain," she replied.

Helen paused, "Let's get something straight, right now. Any member of the bridge crew, can question any order that may put this boat in danger. Any Questions?" All remained quiet. "Very well then. Ensign Crockett, you have the Conn. Station the underway watches. Have the navigator come to the control room."

"Yes Ma'am," Crockett replied. Helen moved to the navigation table and spoke with the Quartermaster. The Navigator arrived.

Lieutenant Westwood addressed the Captain, "Ma'am, you wanted to see me?"

"Yes, Lieutenant. I'd like you to plot a course that will take us around the Republic's fleet to checkpoint Igloo. We must be on station no later than 0200 hours tomorrow night. If we can get there sooner, that would be better." Helen informed him.

"Yes Ma'am," the Lieutenant responded and began his task.

Helen turned to the Conn, "Ensign, adjust your course as directed by the Navigator. I'll be in my cabin." Satisfied that everything was under control, she headed forward.

When Helen reached Bill's cabin, he was reading at his desk. He looked up as she lightly tapped on the door. "Bill, I want you to be Officer of the Deck when we arrive at the SEALs' drop-off point."

"Sure. Any particular reason why?"

"You know more about this boat than anyone else and I want you to take us as close in as possible. I intend to set the nose of this boat in the sand and I think you'd best be able to judge the speed and stopping distance so that we won't get stuck."

"Okay, ma'am, I'll handle it, but it'll cost you," he replied.

"What's the price?" She inquired.

"I'll let you know when the time comes," Bill replied, a big grin across his face.

"Okay, be that way, then. Get some sleep," Helen ordered as she pulled his door shut behind her.

She entered her cabin and closed the door, then lied down on her bunk and was soon sleeping soundly. At 0932 the next morning she was abruptly awakened by an announcement, "BATTLE STATIONS, ALL HANDS MAN YOUR BATTLE STATIONS!" followed by the general alarm. Helen sprang from her bunk, ran out her door and turned aft toward the control room. She encountered a group of sailors coming up the stairs, trying to get to their battle stations and blocking her passage. "Make a hole," she yelled as she pushed through the group. Once in the control room she leaped onto the conn, "What do you have?" She asked Lt. Gorecki.

"Captain, sonar has three destroyers dead ahead. I thought you might want to engage," he replied.

"Negative. What's our present course and speed?"

"We're answering ahead full, steering course one-eight-zero."

"Very well," Helen replied as she thought for a moment. "Pass the word to secure from battle stations." She turned to the Diving Officer, "Dive, come to course two-two-five, increase speed to ahead flank." Meanwhile, Lt. Gorecki passed the word to secure from battle stations over the announcing system. "Lieutenant, maintain this course and speed until we are well past the destroyers. Then have the quartermaster plot a course to bring us back to the base line."

"Yes Ma'am," Gorecki replied, her voice showing disappointment at not engaging the destroyers. She couldn't restrain herself, finally asked, "Captain, why are we running away?"

Helen calmly answered, "Because if we attack, we'll give away our position and that would jeopardize our mission. Now, if there's nothing else, I'll be in my cabin." Helen stepped off the conn and left the control room.

Gorecki replied, "Aye, Aye, Captain."

The rest of the day the Hunley sped through the water toward its destination. As midnight approached, she slowed and cautiously approached the coast. Bill relieved the Officer of the Deck and brought the boat up to periscope depth. Raising the scope and flipping on the night vision lens, he checked in a complete circle around the boat. With nothing in sight, he lowered the scope and took her back down to one hundred feet. He picked up the microphone. "Maneuvering, Conn. Prepare to shift propulsion to impulse drive." Maneuvering replied and Bill sat down to wait the report that they were ready. Soon maneuvering acknowledged they were ready and Bill asked the quartermaster to check the water depth.

"Five-zero feet below the keel," came back. Bill put the mike to his mouth and ordered maneuvering to shift propulsion.

The Throttleman shut off the magnetic drive and turned the knob for the impulse drive motors. He brought them to ahead one-third.

In the control room, Bill waited for maneuvering to report the shift was accomplished, at which time he ordered ahead full. The boat quickly sped up as the sea bottom rushed past and slowly rose toward the boat's keel.

The Quartermaster nervously watched the fathometer as it showed the bottom closing on the boat. Helen and Commander Adamowicz entered just as the Quartermaster announced thirty feet below the keel. Bill welcomed Adamowicz with a smile. "Come on up Commander," Bill beckoned as he waved.

As the Commander stepped onto the conn, the anxious Quartermaster reported, "Two-five feet, Sir!"

Adamowicz quickly picked up on the frightened voice, "Excuse me, XO, but isn't the bottom getting kind of close?"

Bill calmly replied, "Not really, it'll be a lot closer before you leave this boat. You see, we're running a little behind schedule, so I'm trying to catch up."

"Officer of the Deck, two-zero feet below the keel!" The Quartermaster yelled.

"Very well," Bill laughed "Dive, two degree up bubble. Bring us to periscope depth."

The Dive replied, "periscope depth, aye," then relayed the order to the Planesman.

Bill turned to the SEAL, "You ready to go?"

Adamowicz replied, "More than ready."

"Good, we'll be in position in about twenty minutes."

"Thank you for getting us here safely," Adamowicz said to Helen, snubbing Bill.

As Adamowicz started to leave, Bill spoke, "Oh, Commander." The man stopped, but did not turn to look at Bill. "Good luck to you and your team."

The Commander then turned half-around, "Thank you," he said and left.

The Dive announced they were at periscope depth and the Quartermaster added that the bottom was five-zero feet below the keel and rising. "Slow to two-thirds." A report announced the boat was ready to surface and Bill ordered up scope. Grabbing the handles, he made a complete circle and satisfied that the area was clear, he ordered, "down scope. Diving Officer, put us on the surface."

"Aye Sir, Planesman, five degree up bubble. Chief of the Watch, start a low pressure blow on all main ballast tanks, pump the maneuvering tanks overboard."

The boat slowly pushed its way to the surface. The sail broke the surface first, then the bow slowly rose out of the water before settling back onto the surface. Air bubbles surrounded it as air escaped from the bottom of the ballast tanks.

"Officer of the Deck, we are on the surface."

"Very well," Bill responded, "Lookouts to the bridge." The seaman next to the ladder to the bridge started up, opened the hatch and climbed quickly up the ladder. Bill turned towards the navigation center, "Quartermaster, mark depth to the bottom."

The Quartermaster glanced at the fathometer before answering, "Seven-zero feet below the keel, Sir."

"Okay then, let me know when we have twenty feet below the keel. Dive, I am moving to the bridge." Bill quickly went up the ladder into the pitch-dark night. Once topside he opened the watertight box containing the communication equipment. He pressed the talk button, "Control room, this is the bridge, testing." A reply came back signifying that the system was working.

As Bill's eyes adjusted to the dark, he surveyed the ocean around him and could just make out the shore in front of the boat. Faint lights from scattered houses along the shore came into view as they pushed through the water towards them. Suddenly the silence of the night was broken, "two-zero feet of water below the keel." Bill pressed the intercom button, "Open the vents on Main Ballast tank number one." A momentary pause was followed by mist of water shooting up from the forward vents that resembled a whale's blowing. As the water rushed into the bottom vents, the bow slowly sank below the surface. The water rushed over the submerged bow and splashed against the sail, spraying faces of the crew on the bridge. Bill pressed the intercom button, "Control room, slow to one third." The boat began to slow and the spray over the bridge became a light mist.

The intercom again crackled to life, "Bridge, ten feet of water below the keel."

"Very well, all stop. Have the SEALS lay topside through the midship hatch." Bill ordered. He thought for a second before continuing the orders. He switched the intercom controls to the ship's announcing system, "Standby for collision forward." He then hit the red collision alarm switch next to the intercom. Below, the boat was filled with the whooping alarm going off. The watch standers on the bridge could just hear the sound as it flowed up the hatchway. After a couple of tense moments, the bow scraped the bottom. The friction slowed the boat even more until its forward momentum halted abruptly as the bow buried itself into the sand.

Bill looked back at the midship hatch and could barely see the men topside. One man, positioned on his knees next to the hatch, reached inside and pulled out a large package. The two other men took the bundle and laid it in the middle of the deck. Bill could hear the air rushing from the airtank into the raft. Once the raft was inflated, it was tossed over the side and held close by with a line, waiting for the men to enter it. This process was repeated twice more.

The SEALs clambered over the side into the boats and shoved off. Two crewmembers remained topside after they left, but Bill was unable to identify them. Then, one walked toward the sail, but Bill realized it was Helen only after she spoke. "Bill, they're clear. Get us out of here and into deep water, best possible speed."

"Yes Ma'am, but you better get below and dog the hatch first." He replied.

"On my way, Sir," She answered with a laugh.

Once Helen and the other crewmember disappeared through the hatch, Bill ordered, "Conn, this is the bridge. Perform a high pressure blow on #1 main ballast tank, back full." As the air shot into the main ballast tanks, bubbles came up around the hull and the boat slowly moved backwards. The bow popped out of the water and the boat rapidly picked up speed rearward. After several minutes Bill ordered a hard right rudder and all stop. The stern swung to the right and after forty-five degrees, he ordered ahead full. When the boat had all but stopped, Bill ordered a hard left rudder and the boat moved forward with the bow continuing to swing. "Conn, Bridge, steady on course two-eight-five and let me know when we have two-hundred feet below the keel."

The Hunley continued to deep water as the crew watched the SEALs progress towards the beach with a narrow beam of radar. Suddenly the intercom came to life, "Bridge, Control room. We're picking up hostile radar on the EMF, closing fast on the SEALS."

"Damn," Bill muttered. "Bring us about, one hundred-eighty degrees to port. Man the laser fire-control station and have the Captain lay to the bridge." Bill paused and thought the situation through before Helen arrived, which didn't take long.

"What's the problem?" She asked as she crawled onto the bridge.

"We have picked up hostile radar, and the source is headed towards the SEALS. I've changed course and headed back in. I've also ordered the laser fire-control be manned."

"What's your plan?" Helen queried.

"I'd like to go active on radar and attempt to draw the hostiles towards us, then take out what we can before we dive. We need to gain the SEALs ten minutes and they'll be ashore," Bill explained.

As he finished the word came, laser fire-control was manned and ready.

"Very well, Bill, execute your plan. Lookouts below." Helen waited for the lookouts to clear the bridge before she continued. "I'll go below and let you know when we can dive. If it gets too hot up here, lay below. That's an order, mister."

"Yes, Ma'am," Bill replied. "Just make sure you let me know when we can dive."

Helen gave Bill a kiss on the cheek, and then disappeared down the ladder. When she came into the control room, she ordered the Electronics Operator to go active on the radar and tie it into the laser fire-control center.

"Yes Ma'am," the Petty Officer replied and switched the radar from narrow beam to full sweep. "Captain, radar is on full sweep and sending to the laser control."

"Very well," She stepped over to the fathometer, studied it for a couple of seconds, then walked to an intercom box and pressed the bridge button. "Bill, we have full sweep on the radar and eight-zero feet below the keel."

The electronics operator cut in, "Captain, picking up four aircraft. And they've picked up our radar, and are turning toward us. They are definitely hostiles."

"Conn, Bridge, ring up back full." Bill ordered, then leaned down and stuck his head into the hatch so he could talk to the laser operator. "Fireman Johnson, lock onto the lead fighter and fire when ready."

"Yes, sir," she replied. After a brief pause, she continued, "I'm locked on sir, waiting for them to come into range." A few seconds later, "Firing on target one" she said as she pushed the firing button. A distant flash appeared in the night sky as the lead fighter exploded, indicating a direct hit.

"Good. Now lock on another," Bill ordered and the fireman repositioned her targeting cursor.

Before she could get a lock on the target an excited voice came over the intercom, "Bridge, enemy fighters have locked onto us! Three missiles incoming!"

Helen broke in on the intercom, "Bill, clear the bridge, I'm taking her down."

Bill dove into the hatch and shut it behind him. About to climb down the ladder, he heard Fireman Johnson, "XO, I have a lock on one missile and I'm firing." Before Bill could reply she fired at the missile and locked onto the second. As the laser hit the first missile, a brilliant flash lit the night sky. Seconds later, one of the other missiles passed through the explosion and exploded.

The SEALs were landing on the shore as the missiles were destroyed. The flashes flooded them in an eerie glow that lasted only a few seconds, but seemed an eternity. At that point they were exposed and ran at top speed to cover.

As the Hunley's sail slipped below, the third missile impacted the water and exploded. The resulting shockwave rocked the submarine violently and the crew was thrown about. Bill and Fireman Johnson were just coming through the lower hatch when the concussion hit. They were thrown off the ladder, landing in a heap on the deck. As the jolting subsided, Bill looked at Johnson, who was on top of him, and asked her if she was all right. She nodded and rose to her feet. Bill struggled to his feet and almost stumbled onto the conn. He briefly looked at Helen and said, "That was too close. Sorry 'bout that." He picked up the mike. "This is the XO. Check all stations for damage. Make damage reports to the Control Room." He hung the mike up and turned to Helen," Captain, I sure hope we bought the SEALs enough time to make it ashore."

"Radar reported they made landfall while the fighters were engaging us" Helen informed him. After a brief pause she continued, "We've done all we can to help them, so they're on their own. May God be with them."

The phone talker spoke. "Captain, all stations report no structural or mechanical damage, but some minor personnel injuries."

"Very well. Bill, pass the word to secure from battle stations, then have the Navigator plot a course through the Straits of Gibraltar to a point midway between Libya and Italy. We'll go around any hostile ships we encounter. Make sure your relief understands too, okay?" Helen instructed.

"Yes, ma'am," Bill replied in a soft voice, "Go get some sleep."

"Good night." She turned and headed to her cabin.

After Helen disappeared through the door, Bill picked up the microphone and announced, "Secure from battle stations. Set the normal, underway watch, section three. Navigator lay to the control room."

Chapter 17

On the Beach

Adamowicz stood on the beach watching the action. After the explosion on the water's surface, he could barely make out the plane, but a terrible realization hit him, "They're coming at us! Take cover!" he screamed. The SEALs sprang toward anything they could hide behind, and just as the last SEAL dug in, a missile rapidly approached. "Incoming!" he yelled burying his face in the sand and covering his head with his arms. Seconds later the missile detonated on the beach, violently shaking the ground.

The sand rained down, partially burying them. The fighter then opened fire with its machine guns on their position. The trail of bullets raced up the beach, exploding as they hit, marked their path across the sand. One unlucky SEAL chose a wrong spot to hide as bullets cut across his body, causing it to perform a macabre death dance as the plane flashed overhead with a deafening roar.

Adamowicz got to his feet. A quick look around assessed the situation. His men were scattered and disorganized, training can't prepare a man for this. Then he saw the bloody mess a mere ten feet away. Terror crossed his face momentarily and a tear came to his eye, but he quickly regained his composure. He looked at his group, visibly shaken, and shouted orders, "Get your gear! C'mon, let's move out before he gets back! Ski, strip that man's gear," he said, pointing at the unidentified body. He then turned and hurriedly moved away from the ocean, followed by the rest of the team.

Petty Officer Kowalski cautiously approached the bloody body of a man who, a few seconds ago, was a friend and rolled the body over as he fought back the bile churning up his throat. He reached inside the man's shirt, grasped his dog tags, yanked and broke the chain. He kept his head turned away, for he didn't want to see the death mask of his comrade. He decided to wait and read the name later. He reached inside the left shirt pocket and retrieved the man's identification card and stuck it and the dog tag in his shirt pocket. He picked up the dead man's rifle-he wouldn't need it anymore-then turned and ran after the rest of the team.

Ski caught up with the others as they were surveying a small house with a van parked outside. Adamowicz looked at Ski as he approached. "You get everything off Harper?"

Now Ski knew who died and hesitated a second before responding, "Yes Sir." He pulled the card and tag from his pocket pulled out the card and tag and handed them to the Lieutenant.

"Thanks." Adamowicz took them, and put them in his pocket. He and ordered the team to move toward the van. As they reached it, the point man opened the door and slipped into the driver's seat. As he hot-wired the vehicle, the others piled in. Within seconds, the van pulled away from the house and headed down the road towards its destination.

Pentagon

"Mike, stealth bombers will take off for Cuba within the half hour."

"Good, we'll finally get rid of the commies down there. We've let them hang around too long."

"You know, I'm still not convinced they were responsible for the attacks. I don't see any logic in it."

"You really don't?" Steve shook his head. Mike continued. "Now's the perfect time. They're hoping for the Republic's."

"Then why deny it?" Steve cut him off.

Mike leaned back in his chair and thought about the question. He knew he couldn't give his old friend a bullshit answer. "Frankly, I don't know. What I do know, however, is that the attack came from Cuba. That means someone high in their government was involved and if they have those people in the government, it's time to deal with them once and for all! Besides, if we cripple their military, maybe the people will finally rise up and finish the job."

"Alright. You and the President are my bosses and I'll do whatever you say. But, I remember us using this same philosophy against Hussein. It didn't work then, and I doubt it'll work now."

0200 An airbase outside Havana.

"I'm so tired, why do we have to sit up all night. There's no air traffic, nothing on the radar. We should at least be able to take a nap."

"And if the Duty Officer catches you, you're off to prison. Then you'll have plenty of time to sleep until your new boyfriend or a prison guard wants your services."

"Okay, okay. Then I'm going to make my rounds. Maybe the walk will wake me up." The young Corporal rose, left the room. Once outside, he lit a cigar and took a long draw. He looked up just in time to see the missile speeding at him. By the time he realized what was happening, the missile smashed into the tower behind him and the explosion sent him flying across the tarmac landing in a tangle. Unable to move, he helplessly watched the tower slowly crumble and fall, burying him.

High above, a jet streaked through the night sky, the pilot viewing the destruction he created below. He banked right for a moment before he moved the control stick to the left to put his plane in a hard bank to line up for his next run. He watched his infrared monitor until he lined up with the runway and straightened up. A bright flash on the monitor made him look ahead, where the sky was full of bright little sparkles that meant his next run would not be as comfortable as the first. He pulled back on the stick and pushed the throttle to the stop and the plane began a vertical climb to get above the tracers.

The pilot rolled the plane and pushed the nose over to head away from the airfield, as a red light began blinking and an alarm sounded in the cockpit, "Damn it! They've locked on me!" Almost immediately, the light became steady and the buzz changed to an incessant drone. He took a deep breath, "Here we go," and pulled the nose up for another climb. As the missile closed in, he pushed the nose over, released a foil and banked hard right. The missile passed through the foil and lost him. He eased back on the throttle and fought the G-forces to pull the plane through the dive as he turned and headed back to the airport. As he came around he locked onto on the radar station and fired a missile. He then once more, lined up with the runway.

World War III
The Beginning

As he closed on his target, staring at the ground fire blocking his way, he saw fighters pulling onto the runway. "If they get up, I'm dead." He pushed the nose over and eased the throttle forward.

Hurtling toward the target, the planes fire control computer acquired the target and the pilot put it in auto so he could concentrate on flying through the mess ahead. He was only a few feet off the deck when his computer released the payload as the first of the fighters were beginning their takeoff rolls. Two cluster bombs fell and exploded a few feet off the ground, spraying their deadly cargo contents across the airstrip. The pilot glanced in the monitor as his plane was rocked by anti-aircraft fire. The picture showed the bomblets hit the planes during their take off and they exploded.

Almost clear of the anti-aircraft torrent, the battered plane shook violently as one engine burst into flames. He shut it down then increased power to the remaining engine to maintain his speed and altitude. With numerous bullet holes in the plane, it handled like a rock and made the pilot worry if he would make it clear of Cuban waters, much less home. By the time he reached the rendezvous point, the rest of the squadron were on their way home. He switched on his radio and pressed his microphone button. "Tornado, this is Duck, do you copy?" The call was greeted by silence. He tried again, "Tornado, this is Duck, do you copy?" Another moment of silence passed before a reply came back.

"Duck! This is Tornado, we thought you were lost. What kept you?"

"Not much, just a little run in with some AAA and a missile. I'm also down one engines."

"Sounds like you had a rough time. Want company for the trip home?"

"I'd like that very much, in case I have to ditch."

"Is it that bad?"

"She's handling like a truck and I think there's a hole in the fuel tank. My fuel gauge is dropping faster than it should on one engine."

"Roger that. Popcorn, go keep him company, will ya'."

Joel M. Fulgham

"Affirmative Tornado, Hang in there, Duck, I'm on way." Popcorn pulled away from the formation and headed back to escort his stricken comrade.

"Hey, Tornado, Did everybody else make it back?"

"Now that you're here, we have one hundred percent return."

"Hey, you two, I hate to interrupt. This is Popcorn. I have five, repeat, five bogeys coming up behind Duck. I'm going to need help back here."

"Roger that, Popcorn. Okay team; check your fuel tanks, whoever has enough fuel follow me. Duck, push it as hard as you can, bring them to us."

"'Way ahead of you Tornado, It's in the red already, I'm diving to get more speed"

A new voice broke in over the radio, "Hey fly boys, I hate to break into your fun. This is the frigate, U.S.S. McHenry, We have three ships ready to fire on the bogeys. We request you stay clear so we don't hit you by mistake. As soon as Duck's clear, we'll splash them."

"Very well, McHenry, they're all yours. We'll hold here in case they clear you."

The bogeys turned back. "They're running! Thank you, McHenry. We're low on fuel and didn't really want to engage anyway."

"No problem, We've been sitting here waiting, just in case something like this happened. Have a safe trip home."

"Okay guys this is Tornado, head for home."

The first planes of the squadron made it home and waited for Duck and Popcorn. The Base Commander ordered radio communications piped through the hanger so that the entire base could hear. Duck's voice finally came through, "Control Tower, this is Duck. Request emergency landing clearance on runway two-zero."

"Roger, Duck, wind is out of the west-southwest at twenty, visibility is unlimited. The pattern is clear for a straight-in approach on runway two-zero. Radar has you twenty-five miles out on line and on the glide path, emergency crews are standing by."

World War III
The Beginning

"Roger Control, I have a visual on the runway. I do not, repeat do not have an indication of the nose gear being down, I'm not even sure I have one."

"Roger that, Duck, Popcorn, can you get a visual?"

"Control, this is Popcorn, negative on visual, there's to much debris hanging down to see in the dark."

"We will alert emergency crews." The traffic controller looked over his shoulder at the crew chief, who nodded and picked up his radio to inform the emergency crews. The Incident Commander was at the end of the runway with the response team and quickly relayed the information to them.

Back in the tower, "Duck, we have you ten miles out, drifting a little right and a little high."

"Roger tower, trying to correct." The sweat was pouring off Duck as he fought the plane, trying to line up with the runway. He knew couldn't go around to try another landing. For him it was land now or bail out over the ocean. The disembodied voice of the traffic controller again came over his headset, "Duck, we have you five miles out, still drifting right, and too high. Reduce power." Duck pushed on his left rudder pedal with all his strength, but it moved only slightly. The ineffective rudder couldn't bring the plane back into alignment with the runway, so Duck moved the stick and banked it towards the runway. "Duck you're lined up now, but still too high. Reduce power" He pulled the throttle back a little and the plane dropped like a rock. Fifty feet above the ground, he had to throttle up or land short of the runway. The plane slowly increased speed and halted its descent thirty feet above the ground.

"Control tower, this is Duck. I'm coming in hot. I cannot reduce power any further or I'll fall out of the sky."

"Roger. We have you one mile out, on line, below the glide path. There are no building between you and the runway, so you should be okay. Good luck, you have the ball."

Duck could see the lights of the runway rushing at him. His low altitude made him feel he was traveling much faster than he actually was. "Come on baby, we're almost home, hold together, please." As, he passed the end of the runway he cut the throttle and the plane fell from the air as he pulled back on the stick. The main gear hit with a violent thump. Now he had to keep the nose off the ground as long as possible to prevent the plane from flipping. The plane's speed decreased and the nose settled down until the hanging debris made contact with the tarmac. A shower of sparks surrounded the plane as it shuddered briefly and the metal shards tore away, tumbled along the ground. Duck heaved sigh of relief when he realized the nose gear was holding.

He began his long rollout and finally, he pulled into the hanger lights where his comrades got a close look at the plane. The nose was all but gone, the right wing tip was hanging limp and most of the tail was missing. The craft looked like swiss cheese and everyone was amazed that he had been able to fly home, much less land safely.

Chapter 18

On board the Hunley

"Captain on the Bridge!"

"Carry on," Helen said, as she stepped to the Quartermaster table. "Petty Officer Hernandez, what's our position?"

"Five miles due West of the Straits and holding position Captain."

"Very well, Officer of the Deck," She continued as she hopped up on the Con. "Any contacts?"

"Yes, ma'am," replied Lt. Garwacki, looking at the sonar monitors to the left side of the Conn. "We have two confirmed surface contacts five miles past the rocks and a possible submerged contact just behind them."

Helen checked her watch, mumbled. 'Excuse me, Captain?" responded Garwacki.

"Oh, nothing. Just thinking out loud. I'd like a meeting with all off-watch officers in the wardroom in fifteen minutes. Have the messenger make the rounds. I'll be in sonar for a few minutes." Helen stepped off the con and went forward.

Helen turned into the sonar shack. "Sonar Chief, can you get a more definite reading on that submerged contact?"

"Trying Ma'am, but unfortunately those ships we sunk earlier are scattering the signal. That submerged contact could just be reflected sounds from the surface ships. If we keep on patrolling here, we may be able to verify the contacts."

"Okay. You have two hours before nightfall, then we're going in. So do whatever you can."

"Yes Ma'am." Helen left the room and headed to her cabin.

Ten minutes later she was at her desk reading when Bill knocked on the door. "Excuse me Captain, the officers are in the wardroom waiting for you."

"I'll be right there," she replied.

Bill looked at her, puzzled at her appearance, then asked her if she was alright.

"Yes, just trying to figure this out," she replied.

"What's the problem?"

"The best way to navigate the straits without being detected or running into anything. Remember, we sank several ships in the middle of the channel. Now they're preventing sonar from getting a good fix on possible contacts. We know there are two surface ships and sonar thinks there's a submerged contact, but isn't sure."

Bill looked over her shoulder and pointed at the chart, "how about running the northern side of the channel there. It looks like the depth stays over one hundred feet."

"That's what I was thinking, too. It'll be close though, the bottom comes up fast from that point towards the shore. If we're a few feet off course, it could spell disaster. Oh well, we better get going. Don't want to keep them waiting too long," Helen rose from her chair and rolled up the chart. Bill stepped back so she could leave first, then Bill followed through the narrow passageway and down a fight of stairs to the wardroom. As Helen entered, one officer snapped to attention, "Captain on deck."

"As you were." Helen sat down at the head of the table. "First, I want an operational report from each department in two hours. Weapons Officer, load all torpedo tubes and make them ready for rapid fire. Also, run a diagnostic check on the canon. Engineer, I want all air banks charged to full capacity at 0600 hours tomorrow morning. At the same time, be ready to answer all bells through flank speed. Navigator, in one hour and forty minutes we will be running along the north side of the strait. We'll need a precise position before we start 'cause there won't be room for error. Even a few yards off and we could run aground. See me after the meeting. Now, during the next twenty-four hours, we will be the only, repeat, only boat trying to prevent an all-out invasion of Italy and Southern Europe. We will have air support, but it'll be sporadic at best. Our job is to sink as many troop transports as possible and avoid firing at combat ships as long as we can. We want our torpedoes for the troopships. Any questions?" Helen looked around the table. "Very well then, let's get to it, dismissed."

The officers rose and filed out, except for the Navigator, "Okay Captain, where do you want to be?"

World War III
The Beginning

Helen unrolled the chart on the table. "Right here," she said, pointing. "If we start here, we should be able to head due west and stay at a depth of seventy feet."

"Wow, ten feet, that's sure cutting it close."

"You're right, we need someone manning the fathometer the whole time."

"I have the perfect person for that, I'll get right on this."

"There's a catch," Helen added, "We need time so sonar can verify if there's another sub out there."

"Okay, I'll plot a course to get us in position with, say ten minutes to spare."

"Sounds good." Helen rolled up the chart and the two left the wardroom. Helen went to her cabin. As she passed Bill's door, she knocked, waited for an answer. None came, so she opened it and looked inside. Bill wasn't there so she went into her own room, set her alarm clock to awaken her in one hour, then dozed off.

Helen entered the control room as the Quartermaster was informing Bill, now the Officer of Deck, that they were coming to the Navigator's mark for the run. "Very well. Dive, ring up ahead, one-third. On the Quartermaster's mark, come right to course zero-nine-zero. Quartermaster, whenever you're ready."

A hush came over the room as everyone waited for the Petty Officer to give the order. "Diving Officer, begin your turn…now."

"Helmsman, right rudder ten degrees, to a heading of zero-nine-zero," the Dive ordered.

The Helmsman responded, "Right ten degrees, steady on course zero-nine-zero, aye Sir," and turned the wheel. The boat slowly came around to the direction of the strait and the enemy ships awaiting them. The Helmsman slowly returned the rudder the zero position and informed the Dive they were steady on the new course.

The Dive reported to Bill, "Steady on course zero-nine-zero."

"Quartermaster, mark position," Bill ordered.

"Dead on, Sir."

"Very well, good job everyone." Bill then picked up the communication microphone, "Sonar this is the conn, any more information on the submerged contact?"

139

The reply was, "To the best of my ability Sir, I believe there's a submarine there. But, I can't give you a depth or exact location."

Bill looked at Helen. "Well Captain, what do you think?"

"Take us through, Mister. I'll be in sonar and let you know as soon as we've a definite fix on that sub." She turned and headed forward. Bill's eyes followed her as she went the door, then noticed Fireman Johnson at the fathometer, watching him. Bill asked her, softly, "Aren't you supposed to be watching that chart?"

She nodded and fixed her eyes on the screen in front of her.

Bill looked at the Dive Officer, "Dive, all ahead standard, bring us up to Periscope depth."

"Five degree rise on the planes. Chief of the Watch flood negative 5000 pounds." The boat slowly rose until her keel was sixty feet below the waters surface, "zero the planes," He paused a moment to study the depth gauge to make sure they would stay at that depth. "Periscope depth Sir, Maneuvering answering ahead standard."

"Very well. Fireman Johnson, let me know when the bottom is within fifteen feet of us. Quartermaster, if we stray off the plotted course, yell out." Everyone nodded and Bill sat down in his chair, trying to look calm, but he felt beads of sweat on his forehead.

The ship continued in silence for several minutes as Bill kept glancing at his sonar monitor and watched the lines that signaled contacts slowly change positions.

Seaman Johnson finally broke the silence, "Officer of the Deck, bottom is fifteen feet and rising slowly."

"Very well, mark every foot of change from now on," Bill responded as his sweating increased. He looked around at the other crewmembers and saw he wasn't the only anxious one.

"Fourteen feet," came the call. "Steady as she goes," Bill ordered, then stared at the sonar screen. The two surface contacts were becoming more defined, while the submerged contact remained a fuzzy line on the screen.

Seaman Johnson, called out, "Bottom coming up fast," interrupting his thoughts! "Ten feet!"

"All stop!" Bill yelled.

Fireman Johnson continued, "nine feet," she paused, "eight point five feet and holding." Bill sighed as Johnson continued excitedly, "Alright, dropping back down." She paused again, "Thirteen feet now and leveling off."

"Okay. All ahead one third," Bill ordered his eyes strayed again to the sonar screen. Something about the contacts bothered him, but he couldn't put his finger on it.

The quartermaster spoke. "Officer of the Deck, we're now passing Gibraltar."

"Very well," he replied, without taking his eyes off the screen. Fireman Johnson informed him the bottom was slowly dropping away, depth below the keel was back to fifteen feet. "Dive, ring up ahead two thirds." Bill picked up the microphone, "Sonar, this is the XO, please have the Captain pick up the phone." Bill hung the mike up and picked up the phone handset and waited for Helen to answer.

"Yes, Bill."

"Helen, do you have any information on the submerged contact yet?"

"No, we still can't get a good fix on it. We're pretty sure it's a real contact although it's not putting out any screw noise. So, it could be bios"

"Helen, put it on the speaker."

"Sure, hang on." The line went silent momentarily before a hum came over the speaker. Suddenly, Bill figured out why the contact was fuzzy, "Dive, hard right rudder! Bring us to new heading of one-four-zero!" Bill spoke into the phone. "Helen that's an impulse drive unit. I'm taking evasive action."

"On my way." Bill hung up the phone as Helen was coming through the door. She sprang onto the platform. "What actions are you taking?"

"We've changed course to one-four-zero, into the middle of the channel."

"Why? What about the ships?" Helen asked.

"We've passed the rocks, so we should be past them, too. We need deeper water in case we have to do some fancy maneuvering."

"You know were the sub is? How do you know you're not taking us straight to it?"

Bill looked up at the monitor and pointed. "See how this line is still stationary, compared with the surface contacts which have shifted over here" He paused, awaiting her answer. She nodded and he continued. "That contact has to be due east of here, so I'm going south to see if it moves"

"Okay, sounds logical." Helen moved around Bill and sat in the chair. As the boat approached the surface contacts, the fuzzy line began to shift slightly. Helen smiled at Bill, "Damn, you're good. But, don't you think we're getting a little too close to those surface ships."

"Johnson, mark depth to the bottom."

"One hundred fifty three feet, Sir"

"Dive, take her down, to one hundred thirty feet, come left to a new heading of zero-nine-zero, ahead standard." Bill turned to Helen and talked in a softer voice, "Now that we're in, how do we get back out?"

Helen looked at him with that devilish grin, "who said we're leaving."

Before Bill could react to her comment, the boat passed under one of the surface ships and a deafening ping echoed throughout the boat. They looked at each other with apprehension in their eyes. Helen quickly recovered and gave the order, "Ahead flank!"

Before the boat could reach escape speed, the ships above began dropping depth charges. The first two were close enough to rock the sub, but as she rapidly gained speed and moved away from the danger as the explosions grow fainter. "Shit! Now they know we're here!" Helen drew a deep breath. "We have to move on. After midnight, I want to go to four-hour watches. That way, everybody can get some sack time before action starts."

"Captain," Bill asked, "What heading do you want?"

Helen stepped to the quartermaster's station and looked at his chart. "Give me a rough heading for here," she said, pointing at it.

The Petty Officer looked at her, zero-eight-five true."

"Thank you, now plot an accurate course and speed. Then have the Navigator check it." Helen returned to the Con, "XO, new heading is zero-eight-five, ahead full. Anything else?"

Bill smiled and shook his head no.

"Very well then, I'll be touring the ship if anything arises." She leaned close to him. "Stop by my cabin when you get off watch."

"Yes Ma'am."

Chapter 19

At 2340, Helen heard someone knocking at her door, "Who is it?"

"The XO, Captain, reporting as ordered."

"Enter," Bill opened the door. Helen, in a robe was at her desk, reading.

"What would you like, Captain?"

Helen didn't bother to look up, "Did the Navigator give you the course?"

"Yes, Ma'am."

"What's the boat's status right now?" she asked, still not looking at him.

"We're on a heading of zero-eight-three degrees, answering ahead standard. Engineering is charging the air banks, checks on the cannon are complete and all tubes are loaded and ready to fire. Did you turn up anything on your tour?"

"Nothing major, just some storage problems that need to be corrected. Go get a good night's sleep." Bill opened the door, was about to leave when Helen spoke up, "Oh Bill, there's one more thing."

Bill stuck his head through the half-closed door, "Yes Ma'am?"

Helen, stood, slowly untied her belt then pulled the robe open and placed her hands on her hips. "I'd like you to please inspect this, to make sure it's operational for tomorrow."

Bill smiled and stepped back into the room, closing the door behind him. He walked over to her, slipped his arms around her waist and pulled her tight against him. "You're the Captain and I'm here to obey your orders. If it's your wish for me to perform one more inspection, I am willing to carry out that order." He started kissing her on the neck, picked her up and carried her the short distance to her bunk. Then the two lovers fell onto the bunk, locked in each other's loving embrace.

Joel M. Fulgham

0600 the next morning

Helen was sound asleep, dreaming, when she felt the soft press of something on her neck. In a semi-conscience state, she wasn't sure if it was a dream or real. Then, she felt a hand embrace her breast and decided it was time to open her eyes. Slowly they opened. It wasn't a dream. More soft kisses caressed her neck and the hand slowly and softly fondling her. Slowly, she rolled over onto her back and the kisses stopped.

"Good morning, Captain. It is 0600, time to rise and shine."

Helen looked at Bill sitting on the side of her bunk, "Good morning, XO. They never told me during training that wake-up calls could be so nice," she smiled.

"It's my pleasure to serve you, Captain. Now, down to business, radio reports indicate they're ready to start the landings. Early yesterday, some of the transports moved away from the docks while others moved in apparently to take on troops. In addition, two more carriers groups have left Beirut, steaming this way at top speed. However, that's not the worst news. Japan has surrendered and the Republic has declared Israel secured. With the resistance in Israel gone, those forces are now moving through Turkey towards Istanbul. The Pentagon has ordered this operation to be given top priority for assistance from all aircraft within range."

"Bill, why does that worry me?"

"I don't know, could be you don't like the idea of bombs and missiles coming at us."

"I think that's it!" Helen tossed the covers off and sat up. "Please hand me my robe." Bill picked it up off the floor and handed it to her. As Helen put it on she thought over her battle plan. "How soon will the carriers be in range?"

"Best estimate, is late this afternoon. Their fighters will then be able to cover this area."

Helen thought for a moment, "then invasion fleet will move tonight, so let's move south and engage them as they leave port. Then we'll move north and wait for those we miss."

"When we attack, you know, their planes will swarm over that area in a hurry. How far north do you want to move?"

"I was thinking fifty miles, why?"

"Fifty miles? Hmm, that would give us, maybe, two hours before we reengage them. Then add, maybe, fifteen minutes more before their planes locate us."

She paused for a moment, doing her own figuring, "I estimate about an hour-and-half between engagements, then I'd like to be underway ten minutes later. Aircraft will probably cover them after our first attack and they'll know, by then, that they can't find us using passive sonar, so they'll use sonar buoys ahead of the fleet. We'll have to find a good thermal layer to hide under while we wait. Oh well, we'll worry about that when the time comes. Meanwhile line us up for the first attack."

"Yes Ma'am, will do." Bill stood and took a step toward the door, then paused and looked back at Helen, "You know, you should get some sleep, too." He left.

USS Hunley 1813 hours local time

"Captain on the bridge!"

"Carry on, XO, status!"

"Captain, we have a large concentration of ships coming out of Tripoli harbor, range five miles and closing at thirty knots, at fifteen degrees, relative."

Helen stepped up onto the conn and scanned the sonar monitor. "Looks like one massive armada."

"That would be the destroyer screen, Captain. We're below a thermal layer, waiting for them to pass. They just completed a zag maneuver that brought them to a heading towards us. I think they'll probably zig at about the three mile mark and head off in this direction," Bill pointed at the sonar screen marking a line that would lead them farther to the west. "I request we man battle stations."

"Very well. Phone talker, pass the word to man battle stations. Messenger of the watch, make rounds in berthing and have everyone man their battle stations."

The phone talker relied the message as the messenger moved off.

"Okay, Bill, I have the Conn, you take fire control."

"Yes, Ma'am." Bill stepped down and to the fire control.

More personnel filed into the Control Room and took their battle stations.

The phone talker spoke, "Captain, the Communications Officer has picked up signals that fighters and bombers are inbound from both sides. Our fighters are moving to intercept the Republic's planes, while the bombers are continuing on to the fleet. Also, operation 'Greenbay' is underway and operation 'Squeeze' is starting up."

"Very well. Navigator, I want you to continually plot and update a course to Zwara."

"Zwara, Ma'am?"

"Yes, Nav, Greenbay is a rescue mission for the crew of the Greenbay. Intelligence has it that the crew was not all lost, but taken prisoner. That's where the SEALS went. When the rescue is complete, we'll pick up survivors off the coast of Zwara."

"Captain, the destroyers are turning to port."

"Range?"

"Three point five miles."

"Bill, you were off by a half mile, shame on you."

"Excuse me, I said about three miles, three point five is about."

"Alright, I'll let it slide this time. Dive, bring us to a heading of one-eight-three, ahead one third."

"Conn, Sonar. More contacts, bearing one-eight-zero," came over the intercom.

Helen picked up her microphone and punched up sonar, "I have it on my screen, mark the range."

"Working," come the reply.

Helen waited, for what seemed a lot longer than the fifteen seconds that actually passed, before she asked again, "Sonar, Conn, mark range."

"Range to nearest target four miles."

"XO, you get that?"

"Yes, Ma'am, target identified and locked in as number one target."

World War III
The Beginning

"Continue identifying new targets as you make them out, designate one torpedo for each. If we don't sink it, we can at least damage it and make it an easier target for the bombers."

An excited voice came over the intercom, "Conn, Sonar. New sonar contact bearing one hundred degrees, relative."

Helen looked at her monitor as she picked up her mike, "Sonar, Conn. Can you identify?"

"Yes Ma'am, contact is submerged, moving in at estimated fifty knots. "It's the submarine we blew past coming through the Straits."

"Very well, Sonar." Helen looked around the control room before fixing on Bill. "Navigator, are there any undersea mounds in the area?"

"None close enough to the surface to interfere with maneuvering."

"XO, lock the canon fire control on the submarine, when it gets in range we'll come around ninety degrees and fire."

Bill glanced at the fire control screen before answering, "Captain, they'll be in range before the transports are."

Helen checked her monitor again before answering, "You're right, Dive, come left to new heading one-six-five, ahead two-thirds."

"Coming left to new heading one-six-five, engineering answering ahead two-thirds."

"XO, we'll slide behind the destroyers and shoot from the other side, facing the submarine."

"Very well, Captain, the canon is locked on target."

The Hunley sped through the water toward the destroyers moving northeast. "XO, when we pass under the destroyers open the inner and outer torpedo tubes and prepare to fire."

"Aye, aye, Captain. All torpedo tubes are locked onto targets one through twelve."

"Conn, Sonar, change in target acoustics, they are turning."

Helen quickly grabbed you mike, "Which way, Sonar?"

A short pause greeted her as the sonar operators listen, "Toward us."

"Dive, all stop!"

The Diving Officer reached down and turned the engine order telegraph to the stop position, "Engineering answering all stop."

"Everybody, cross your fingers and hope their sonar misses us." The room was extremely quiet as everyone held their breath, waiting for the destroyers to pass above. After several tense moments, the silence was broken as a short high-pitched ping echoed through the boat and everyone waited for another to follow. After a few moments, the phone talker broke the silence, "Captain, Sonar reports the destroyers are still moving away."

Helen drew a heavy deep breath and exhaled, "That was close, Bill, open inner and outer tube doors. Dive, ahead one third." Helen looked at the sonar monitor, "Sonar, Conn, where's that sub?"

"We don't know Captain, it disappeared."

"Damn! They must of heard that ping and stopped too. They're coasting just like we did," she said as she looked over at Bill, who was turned from the fire control system.

"Captain, we need to come around to a heading of one-eight-seven to get into firing position. The transports are coming into range."

Helen paused as she thought for a moment, "Dive, come right to heading of two-seven-five."

"Captain, that's not correct."

"XO, this is my boat, I know what I'm doing!" Helen looked down at the deck and took a deep breath before looking back at Bill. "Sorry, we'll continue with the original plan, However I want to be in position to fire as soon as we reacquire that submarine."

"Yes, ma'am, sorry."

"No problem. Just make sure I'm not missing something."

Bill turned back to the fire control console, "Captain, all tubes are open and ready to fire. Targets one through twelve are locked into the fire control console. Three targets are in range."

"Very well. Standby for firing point procedures." Helen stood watching her sonar screen, looking for any trace of the hunter to which they were the prey. "Navigator, plot a course for the hostile submarine, based on their last-known position and heading. Figure that they killed propulsion and coasted, maintaining the heading they were on."

World War III
The Beginning

"Yes, ma'am. Quartermaster, calculate the coasting distance of an alpha class submarine with initial speed of fifty knots."

The quartermaster turned to his computer, brought up information on alpha class submarines and entered the data. The computer rapidly returned the needed information. The quartermaster walked to the chart table, picked up a compass, adjusted it and began marking on the chart.

"Captain, all targets are within range."

"Very well, XO begin firing."

"All tubes verified open, firing solutions are verified, ready to fire tubes one through twelve."

"Very well, here we go, firing tubes one through twelve at five second interval."

"Fire tubes one through twelve, five second intervals, aye." Bill pressed the fire button, and the noise of air pushing the launching ram filled the boat as it forced water into the torpedo tube and pushed the torpedo out into the ocean. Once clear the tube, the torpedo's engine started and propelled it toward its target." Five seconds later the procedure was repeated as the second torpedo was away.

"Captain, we have a possible location for that sub! We're in range!

Just then a frantic voice came over the intercom. "Conn, Sonar, torpedo in the water! Close in starboard!"

"Dive, ahead full, crash dive, launch counter measures, hard to port!" The boat rapidly gained speed as the torpedo closed on her. The counter-measures bubbled in the water to confuse the sonar of the deadly object speeding in. The torpedo headed into the cloud of bubbles and detonated. The Hunley was violently rocked by the explosion close astern. As the shock wave died, Helen spoke to the phone talker, "Phone talker, get damage reports!" She then addressed Bill, "XO, how many torpedoes did we get off?"

"Five, Captain. Fifteen seconds left on the run for the first one."

"Conn, Sonar, We lost the towed array," came an announcement over the intercom.

"Damn, what else can go wrong?" Helen quickly thought over her options. "Dive, come left to zero degrees, bring us back up to two hundred feet, slow to two thirds." She picked up the mike, "Sonar, Conn, turn the gain on forward scanning sonar as high as you can. Find that submarine! Bill, watch your fire control monitor. As soon as you get anything, hit it with the cannon."

"Yes Ma'am, We have detonation on the first target." Bill informed Helen just as the shock wave was gently rolling the Hunley. Four more gentle rolls followed as the other torpedoes found their marks.

As the ship came around, the sonar monitors began picking up multiple inbound contacts. "Captain, it looks like the destroyers are coming back."

"I see them, XO. I make out five, do you concur?"

"Yes Ma'am, five contacts. But without the towed array we have no range data."

"Use your best guess then, lock on the targets and fire when ready."

"Captain, I request we proceed to periscope depth and get a quick visual fix on the targets."

"Request denied, use your best guess."

Bill nodded a reply to the Captain and fed the limited information into the fire control computer. In a few minutes he spoke up, "we have solutions on the targets, ready to fire torpedoes six through ten."

"Fire when ready."

"Captain, I have an idea. Can we change course fifteen degrees?"

"Why?"

"The computer maybe able to use change in direction to the targets to determine the range."

"Very well, Dive come right fifteen degrees for five minutes, then come back to a heading of three-five-five degrees. Bill, you have five minutes."

"Thank you Captain." Bill watched for the range display for the firing solution. Finally one-by-one the ranges filled in. "Captain, we have the ranges to the targets. They're all out of range, but will be in range in about one minute." Bill paused for a moment and glanced at his sonar display. "Captain, look at the sonar, there's the sub, following in the wake of the middle destroyer."

"We have her. Bill, lock on tube twelve. If she runs, we will close in and use the cannon."

"Yes Ma'am, targeting solution being fed for tube twelve. Tubes one through five indicate reloaded and ready to fire."

"Captain, we have reached the five minute mark, turning to heading of three-five-five degrees."

"Very well."

"Conn, Sonar, We're picking up active sonar."

"Captain, targets are in range."

"Very well, fire twelve, then six through eleven, rapid fire, get them out as fast as possible. They'll be returning fire as soon as they lock on us."

"Yes, ma'am, beginning rapid fire." Bill pushed the fire buttons at approximately two-second intervals. The torpedoes left the boat and sped through the water towards their targets.

The noise generated by the fired torpedoes disrupted sonar's contact with the enemy vessels. They could only hear close-in loud contacts. New contact reports came over the intercom, "Torpedoes in the water, inbound!"

"Ahead full, full rise on the planes! Bring us up to one hundred feet launch counter measures. Bill, you still have a lock on the sub?"

"Yes, Ma'am, they'll be in cannon range in thirty seconds."

"Conn, Sonar, torpedoes are changing depth, still heading straight for us."

"Damn it! Dive hard to port, ahead flank!" The boat banked into the turn as she came about and gained speed.

"Captain, they must have changed the torpedo targeting from sonar to magnetic. If that's so, if we go dead in the water, the torpedoes won't be able to lock on us."

"How do we get out of their path?"

"I recommend killing propulsion dive and turn."

"Very well. Dive, all stop and bring us back to our attack heading, make your depth two hundred feet." Helen picked up her mike, "Sonar, Conn. We're coming around, find that sub ASAP."

As the boat was turning, five of their torpedoes found their mark and sent sound waves through the water.

After a few moments the 'Dive' announced the boat was on their original attack heading. The Control Room was deadly quiet as everyone waited to hear the target had been acquired. "Captain, it looks like two of the destroyers have been disabled and are dead in the water. The other three are still coming, but two at reduced speed."

"Very well," Helen replied. The destroyers weren't her main concern at the moment. It was that other submarine. Her Captain had foiled the Hunley's two previous attacks and degraded her boat's battle readiness. Helen almost regretted having to sink such a worthy adversary. Then after a long several minutes, the announcement came over the intercom, "Conn, Sonar. Target acquired, they appear to be closing on a parallel course, range is calculating."

"Very well," she responded. "Bill feed the data into the cannon fire control."

"Captain, we have a solution and range. We need to come left twenty degrees to be in firing position."

"Very well. Dive, come left twenty degrees. Bill, fire when ready."

"We have a positive lock, Firing!" The lights dimmed as the cannon charged and released its deadly energy. As the shock waves from the exploding submarine returned to the Hunley, she rolled with the dissipating wave. "Got it!"

"Dive, ahead full, take us down to five hundred feet."

"Conn, Sonar. Sounds like the destroyers are dropping depth charges ahead."

The Dive turned and looked at Helen expecting her to change the orders. "Dive, carry out your orders."

The Hunley passed deep below the destroyers, the depth charges exploding around her. The blasts rocked the boat, but none were close enough to cause serious damage.

Chapter 20

The Communications Officer came through the door and handed a paper to Helen, "Captain, we just received this."

Helen read the paper, then looked toward the Quartermaster, "Quartermaster, what's the heading and run time for Zwara?"

The Quartermaster checked the chart and plotted a course from their current position to Zwara. "Heading is two-four-five degrees and running time is one-hour-and-forty-minutes at ahead, full."

"Very well," Helen picked up the microphone. "Sonar, Conn. We're closing in on the convoy again. Let me know when you have a lock on eight ships." Helen turned to Bill. "How many tubes are ready to fire?"

Bill looked at his monitor, "eleven are loaded. The last fish is being loaded right now."

The intercom crackled, "Conn, Sonar. We have six ships as firm contacts. We also have aircraft dropping sonar buoys."

"XO, feed the data into the computer. Diving Officer, bring us up to two hundred feet."

Bill busily worked the fire control computer, trying to nurse the firing solutions and ranges. Finally, he turned to Helen, "Captain, there's not enough angle to the targets to calculate range. We need to change course fifteen degrees to get some angle difference."

"Dive, come left fifteen degrees." Bill watched and made some adjustments until the ranges filled in.

The intercom came alive, "Conn, Sonar. We're picking up noises that sound like something big hitting the water."

"XO, apparently the air battle's underway. You ready to fire?"

"Ready to fire on six targets. Targets seven and eight won't be in range for another minute."

"We'll have to settle for six. Commence firing and let's get out of here, the SEALs will be waiting."

"Yes Ma'am, Firing tubes one through six." Bill once again pressed the fire buttons in series. "All six fish away and running."

"Very well. Dive, come to a heading of two-four-five ahead full." Just then, the boat filled with rapid high-pitched pings. They'd had been found! "Full dive on the planes, ahead flank!" The boat responded as her bow rapidly dropped so the deck was pitched at a forty-five degree angle.

"Conn, Sonar. We have incoming depth charges and torpedoes."

"Launch counter measures, all stop." Inside the Hunley the noise of exploding depth charges could be heard, each one a little closer. Then a high-pitched whine filled the boat as a torpedo sailed by, narrowly missing the coasting boat. As the speed of the boat slowed, the diving planes lost their bite and the boat's bow rose, resulting in a slower descent into the safety of the deep.

"Captain we just passed through a thermal layer." This announcement was accompanied by a very noticeable decrease in the intensity of the pinging.

"Dive, ahead two-thirds. Level off at six hundred feet." The Hunley pulled away from the explosions that threatened her. The Control room remained in silence for another fifteen minutes until Helen assumed the attackers had lost them, "Dive, ahead full. Helen picked up her mike again. "Attention all hands, this is the Captain speaking. Thank you for carrying out your duties so well. We have also successfully carried out our mission, engaging the enemy fleet. However, I cannot be sure how many ships we sank or disabled, but the Republic will certainly feel our efforts. We now have one more mission to complete, then we'll head stateside for some well-deserved rest and maintenance. I think it's safe to say that this is the only sea trial in history that actually involved combat. Thanks to you and the design abilities of our Executive Officer, the Hunley has proven herself to be the finest submarine ever built. Now secure from battle stations." Helen hung up the mike and turned to Bill. "You take the Conn, continue running deep for another half-hour, then go to periscope depth and take a quick star shot, just to make sure our navigation equipment wasn't damaged. Then, take her back down to one hundred feet and continue to the rendezvous coordinates. I'll be touring the boat."

*World War III
The Beginning*

Helen left the Conn as Bill took over. She went through the boat, shaking hands with her crew and thanking everyone she saw.

2330 hours USS Hunley off the coast of Zwara
Bill was looking through the periscope and saw an object in the distance. He zoomed in on it. "Dive, prepare to surface. Chief of the Watch, raise the snorkel mast. Then he picked up his microphone and announced, "Prepare to surface without air. Station the small boat retrieval party at the machinery room hatch. Laser gunner, lay to the Control Room"

Helen, in her cabin, heard the announcement. She glanced at the clock on the wall. "I wonder if he'll be with them," she mumbled, then rose and headed aft to join the retrieval party.

Bill continued issuing orders, "Chief, start the blower on all main ballast tanks. Dive, up five degrees on the planes." As the air forced it's way into the ballast tanks the water was expelled and the boat slowly rose from beneath the water. Several minutes later, the Diving Officer reported they were on the surface. "Chief, equalize pressure in the boat."

"Pressure is equal."

"Phone talker, tell the retrieval party to lay topside. Dive, I am moving to the Bridge. Lookouts to the Bridge."

The two seaman standing by moved to the ladder, opened the hatch and disappeared through the opening. Bill followed them up. Once on the bridge, he looked aft and saw the members of the retrieval party emerging from the hatch. He then looked toward shore to where he had seen the rafts. One lookout announced they were about fifty yards out.

"Let me see." The lookout handed his night binoculars to Bill who looked over the ocean. He handed the binoculars back to the lookout. Looking aft, he recognized Helen standing next to the hatch and called to her: "Captain, I make out six rafts!"

"Bring us to them, ahead slow!" Helen's heart beat faster as she wondered again if he made it.

On the bridge, Bill ordered the course correction. The bow swung to port and the Hunley closed the gap to the rafts. When they were close enough to make out with the naked eye, Bill ordered all stop and the oarsmen on the rafts finished the trip on their own.

The first boat pulled alongside and a SEAL tossed a rope to a crewmember. One-by-one the crewmembers helped the men off the rafts. Some of the rescued Greenbay crew, due to the hardship they endured, could barely walk; much less pull themselves out of the rafts. One-by-one, the injured were lowered down the hatch to waiting medical help.

Helen checked the rafts for Matt. Finally, the last rafts pulled alongside, and her heart sank. There was still no sign of him. Adamowicz, yelled from the raft, "This man needs surgery, in a hurry!" He pointed at a figure in the bottom of the raft, Helen identified him as an officer. As they rolled him over to lift him out of the raft, she saw his face and gasped. "Good Lord, Matt!" She looked at Adamowicz, "What happened?"

"He went to look for crew members we couldn't reach. He was shot leading them back to us."

The crew lowered him down the hatch and Helen yelled to the bridge, "Bill, as soon as we've cleared the deck, get us out of here, flank speed." Helen then went down the ladder, followed by Adamowicz and the other crew members who were topside.

From the sail, Bill saw the hatch close, "Clear the bridge!" The two lookouts quickly disappeared down the hatch with Bill close behind. Once more in the control room he ordered, "Prepare to Dive!"

"The board is green, sir."

"Very well. All head two-thirds, take her down, open all vents, five degree down bubble. Make your depth one hundred feet and come to a new heading two-nine-zero." The orders were carried out and the boat sank back below the gently rolling Mediterranean Sea.

"Officer of the Deck, we are steady at one hundred feet, heading is two-nine-zero degrees."

"Very well, ahead flank. We're going home!"

Back in the Corpsman's office Helen spoke, "Doc, I have the crew setting up the wardroom for surgery, can you do this?"

"Captain, he doesn't have a choice. If I don't stop the bleeding, he'll die."

"What can I do to help?"

World War III
The Beginning

"Go through the medical records and pick out the ones with A-positive blood. The Commander's going to need a lot of it. So, we need as many people as possible as donors."

A crewmen stepped to the door, "Doc we're ready."

Helen said, "Go, take care of him."

The young Petty Officer, "Doc," knew this would be the biggest challenge of his young life. With no surgical training, he would hold a man's life in his hands. He stepped into the wardroom's galley, scrubbed up, then entered the wardroom and looked at the man on the table. Satisfied that all was ready, he slowly moved to the table and bowed his head in prayer.

A half-hour later, Helen finished going through the medical records and contacted the crewmembers with the needed blood type. All agreed to supply the precious blood needed, and reported to the wardroom galley. She stepped into the Control room and to the Conn. "Bill, Any word yet?"

"No Ma'am, but in this case, no news is good news. We're coming up on the Strait. Do you want to run it or wait here until after the surgery?"

"Any contacts?"

"Yes, two."

"Ring up all stop and wait. We don't want to rock the boat now."

"Dive, all stop. Station keeping." Turning back to Helen, "Captain, what are your orders?"

"Stay on station until Doc's finished. Then take us through as fast as possible. Have the Nav plot us a course to New London."

"Alright. Why don't you go get some sleep? You look beat."

"No thanks. I'll sit outside the wardroom and wait."

Helen left and Bill watched her leave.

Three-and-half hours into the surgery, Helen still waited in the passageway outside the wardroom, her head against the bulkhead, dozing. The door opened and so did her eyes. Doc stepped out, surprised to find her there. "How is he?" She anxiously queried.

He took a deep breath before speaking, "I think he'll make it. He's not out of the woods, but he's got a fighting chance."

"Can I go in?"

157

"He's still out, but you can see him."

"Thank you, Doc." Helen started in, stopped and turned to Doc. Please tell the XO to get us out of here." The Corpsman nodded and walked away as Helen entered the room. Inside, she stood and looked at Matt for a long time before stepping to his side and looking down at him. A tear streamed down her cheek, she pulled a chair to the table, sat down and held his hand.

Bill navigated the Hunley through the Strait and after they were clear, went to the wardroom to check on Matt. As he entered, he was shocked to see Helen holding Matt's hand, asleep with her head resting on the table. He gathered himself and walked up behind her. Gently, he placed his hand on Helen's shoulder and she woke with a start and looked at Bill. "You okay?" He asked.

"Yeah, I think so. Where are we?"

"On our way home."

"Any problems getting through the Strait?"

"No." Bill looked at Matt and said, "but we need to find a place to put him."

"We'll put him in my cabin." She responded.

For the next two days, Helen stayed by Matt's side, holding his hand and sleeping in a chair at his side. Bill kept her informed of the boat's progress and relayed her orders to the crew. Finally, the boat pulled into Groton, for some much-needed rest for the crew and long overdue permanent repairs. The boat and crew had performed magnificently since they had put to sea for trails but had to go into combat before being fully tested.

Matt was placed on a stretcher and maneuvered through the tight confines of the boat, then carefully lifted up through the main hatch. Bill stood next to Helen as they watched the still-unconscious Matt carried off the boat and into the waiting ambulance. As it drove away Helen turned to Bill, "Bill, you have Command. I have to go to a debriefing with the Commodore. Get the off-duty personnel off the boat as soon as possible. Tomorrow the Admiral will be here to decorate the crew, so make sure everyone knows they have to be in dress whites, clean shaven and have their hair cut."

Helen turned to leave. Bill reached out and gently grasped her arm, "Helen", he said softly, "Is there anything I can do or say?"

World War III
The Beginning

Helen said with a tear in her eye, "Just give me a little time to work this out. I thought he was dead and now I just don't know."

Bill let her arm go and she left the boat and headed down the pier toward the Tender.

The End

Joel M. Fulgham

About the Author

Joel Fulgham grew up in a small town in Tennessee. He served in the US Navy for eight years. During that time he served on two SSBN submarines and a submarine tender. Joel currently resides in the Chicago suburbs with his wife and two daughters. He has been employed at Fermi National Accelerator Laboratory since 1991.